STEALING VEGAS

VANESSA M. KNIGHT

Stealing Vegas

Copyright © 2023 by Vanessa M. Knight

Published by Inked Publishing

Cover Art © 2020 by Qamber Designs & Media

Edited by Nancy Canu

The characters and events portrayed in this book are fictitious. Any similarity to real persons, living or dead, or events, is coincidental and not intended by the author.

ISBN: 978-1-7344206-2-3

ACKNOWLEDGMENTS

As I finish up Shay's book, I wanted to acknowledge the work of own voice authors. Diversity is a big part of life in Chicago and writing the Chicago's finest series has been an absolute joy. However, I wouldn't want to take away anyone's voice.

Shay started as Joe's partner, but as I got to know her and her family in the first two books, I found I absolutely loved her. She was in my mind, wanting to get her own story. And I believe that she deserves her happily ever after. I truly hope you enjoy Shay's journey. And if you are looking for own voice books that can speak to an authentic experience, I'm including a few of my favorites. I hope you'll give them a shot.

Hollywood Ending ....Kellye Garrett
    Better than Fiction...................Alexa Martin
    Crazy on You ....Crystal B. Bright
    Drunk on Love ....Jasmine Guillory
    Act Your Age, Eve Brown......Talia Hibbert
    When No One is Watching ......Alyssa Cole
    Her Seductive Dare............Lena Hart
    Hot Under His Collar..Andie J. Christopher

PROLOGUE

THE DIAMOND NECKLACE fell to the ground with a clink. "Dammit."

Fifty seconds.

He needed to be more careful. He picked up the necklace and dropped it in the bag on the counter. His fingers squished as he pulled a tray of rings from the open safe deposit box. It was the damn latex gloves. These vaults were so damn hot.

Diamonds. Rubies. Gold. Twenty rings worth probably about a hundred grand. More than he'd make in a year—and he was making it in one fucking night.

He pulled the gold bands from the velvet-covered foam and dropped them into the bag. Each clink was another couple thousand dollars toward his retirement. Another thousand dollars toward his freedom.

Forty seconds.

He checked the open box. Nothing. Nothing left. Turning to the wall of boxes, he yanked number 4518 from its slot and slammed the box on the counter, knocking the first one to the floor.

Thank fuck the casino didn't have noise sensors.

Twenty seconds.

He looked up at the security cameras panning back and forth—seeing nothing. They saw, but all they saw was a masked man. And the security guards were too busy dealing with a drunk and disorderly.

He'd made sure of it.

This vault was guarded almost 24/7, so the hard part of the night was staying away from employees. The attendant's midnight potty-break was his only window. His only chance.

He pulled out a stack of cash and a gold watch. Nice.

The take for tonight was totally worth it.

Ten seconds.

He grabbed the bag and walked out of the vault door. His fingers itched to take off the gloves and the mask. Not yet. Not till he was safely away from the cameras and the glitter of the Vegas Strip.

CHAPTER ONE

SHAYLEIGH WASHINGTON STOOD next to her bag at the luggage carousel and watched suitcase after suitcase crawl past. Not that anyone called her Shayleigh. Hell, she didn't know if anyone even knew that was her real name. She'd never gotten close enough to anyone to tell them. Anyway, Shayleigh was too girly for a detective with the Chicago Police Department.

Her partner's girlfriend Brook yelled from the other side of the carousel. "Shay, watch out!"

Shay attempted to turn. The air knocked from her lungs when a body barreled into her back. She twisted and grabbed the hit-and-run asshole's coat as he tried to whip past her.

"Washington, what the hell are you doing?" Detective Marco Lopez tried to pull away. "My bag is about to disappear." He squirmed, slipping from her grip, and Shay managed to not nose-dive into the floor.

Lopez ran to the luggage carousel, jumping onto the conveyer belt. He stepped over bag after bag, hopping an arm reaching for another suitcase. He missed the arm but tripped over a dark green duffel. By some miracle, he didn't fall off the conveyer and hit himself in the head. Although the people who almost lost a limb looked about ready to take off said head.

He grabbed his suitcase and held it high in triumph as the conveyer inched back toward Shay. He jumped down, right in front of her—right where he'd jumped onto the belt a little over a minute ago. Bag in hand, he smiled and walked toward the exit.

"Dammit, Lopez." Shay twisted her neck as she followed. "Those things go in a circle. Like around. Like, wait until it comes back and then grab your stuff."

"Sorry. But who's got time to wait for the bag to come all the way back around?" Lopez dropped the bag he'd just trampled innocent people for and turned, opening his arms wide. "The women of Vegas await."

If Lopez made it back home to Chicago in one piece, it would be a freaking miracle. A four-hour flight and one almost face-plant later, she was ready to slap the Puerto Rican right off the face of her annoying coworker.

"Washington, Casanova, hold up. I'm still waiting for my bag," Joe Perretti yelled over to Shay and Lopez. Perretti was Shay's partner, and after dealing with Lopez today, she wanted to give the chief back home a bag of candy for pairing her with Perretti. If she had to deal with Lopez on a daily basis...ugh.

He was a good cop, but his personal life was a train wreck of crab-ridden badge bunnies—and he liked to share his exploits. Shay could think of a million other things she'd rather listen to than how long it takes to get rid of crabs. Forty-eight hours, in case anyone was wondering.

But he was young. Everyone did stupid things in their youth. Since she'd been raising her brother at the time, her period of stupidity was limited to an ill-fated marriage. But everyone expressed their idiocy differently.

She grabbed her phone and sent a quick text to her brother and Gran that she'd landed even though they told her not to text. Her phone buzzed right back with a text from Gran. *Just have fun.* With everything going on back home, how was she supposed to do that?

She tilted her neck and massaged the airline-seat crick from her shoulders—and all thoughts of everything back home behind. This was her chance to forget it all.

"What are you doing?" Lopez snuck up behind her, pouting as he stared out the glass doors to a side street in Las Vegas. He looked like a cat watching a squirrel flaunt its freedom. All he needed to do was press his face to the glass.

"What does it look like I'm doing? I'm stretching. Some of us didn't spend the whole flight jumping around the plane trying to hook up with the flight attendants."

He'd batted those long eyelashes at the women and followed them to their little kitchen. Up. Down. Up. Down. In his seat. The seat next to her. He was a horny little jack-in-the-box. Did she mention it was a long freaking flight?

"The redhead was hot, and did you see the way she looked at me? I was so in."

"Yeah, she was hot." Shay could admit the redhead was hot if a person was into red hair. And women. Shay was into neither. Give her a man with dark hair and dark eyes any day of the week. If she were looking for a man.

She pulled a bottle of moisturizer from her carry-on. It seemed the older she got, the drier her skin became. She squirted some on both arms and rubbed it in, watching as the lotion filled in the grayish cracks, her skin slowly morphing back to its usual rich brown. Tucking the bottle away, she walked toward the doors. Sunshine. Air. She couldn't wait to breathe something other than that recycled stuff in the aircraft.

And walking out the doors would have the added bonus of her being outside, alone, in the quiet. The whine of the airplane gone. The yapping of Lopez and all the voices in the cabin gone. No one to hear her sigh or ask her why the air was dragging from her lungs. She didn't want to think about how tired she was. She didn't want to think about how bad she needed this vacation.

Vacation. *Hah.* This was a job with a vacation thrown in. Her wallet liked the arrangement, but her psyche was questioning the whole situation.

Lopez followed her. "Where the hell are you going?"

Away from him and the discussion about the redhead, and what exactly he meant by *in.* She skipped all that with a simple "Outside."

"So, I was saying. The redhead. She had a tight little—"

"Really? I don't want to know about her tight places..." Okay. Wrong wording. So wrong.

"I didn't get a chance to see *all* her tight places." Lopez waved a tiny napkin. "But when she calls me tomorrow, I hope to fix that."

Ick. Wasn't the conversation about the flight attendant over? Shay was over it. The one drawback of being one of the guys? The guys told you things that you really didn't want to hear. Sex life, injuries. The most important thing she learned working with men was if they said *look at this*...don't. The more excitement in their voice, the grosser the view.

The same rule applied to eating mysterious things. And don't get her started on "smell this." Why, on all that was holy, did anyone ever want to share a smell that was horrid?

Couldn't they keep some of the mystery in their relationship?

"I think I sat on my balls." Lopez adjusted his shorts as he lifted his knees, walking like a peacock.

Apparently not. The only bright spot was that when she got back to the city she'd be starting her new job as Lieutenant of Forensics. No more ball stories. Bittersweet happiness burst inside her chest and made it ache. No more stories.

New Job. New division. Alone. No friends. It had taken her ten years to find these friends and soon they'd be gone. One more thing she didn't want to think about today.

"Shut it, Lopez." Shay's partner, Joe Perretti, walked toward the exit, his arm draped over his girlfriend. "No one wants to hear that shit." Brooklyn Southby giggled as she tossed her blonde hair over her shoulder and kissed his neck. Thankfully the two had sat a few rows up on the plane. The kissy-face and hand-roaming was something Shay didn't need to watch up close and personal.

"I'm keeping it real, bro," Lopez shot back. "I got issues."

Definitely not arguing that.

They stepped out into the desert heat. Dry heat. Heat that burrowed deep into your bones. Definitely better than the seventies she left back in Chicago. Seventy in June. What the hell was that about?

The sun beat down, reflecting off the cars idling in front of the entrance. Squeals and laughter rang through the air as travelers dumped their suitcases into limos and taxis. A stretch limo on steroids stood by the curb. Big. Black. An SUV—with an erection. A woman stood in front of an open door holding a sign that had *Brook & Chicago's Finest* written in Sharpie.

Nice. Chicago detective Adam Byrnes had flown out earlier in the week, saying he'd take care of everything. Including the limo. After all, they were in town to guard the jewelry for Adam's family company. A limousine ride to the hotel was probably just the first step of this crazy trip.

Brook walked up to the woman in a black suit and shook her hand. "Hi, I'm Brook."

The woman tucked the sign under her arm and opened the back door. "Welcome to Vegas."

"Hell yeah." Lopez slid into the gaudy bus and stuck his head out the door. "I am Chicago's finest. I don't know how the rest of you are getting to the hotel." His head flopped against the headrest as he groaned. "I could totally get used to this."

The rest of the finest jumped onto the white leather seats, ignoring Lopez and his bliss-filled groans. It was nice. Not just nice—very nice. Shay slid her hand over the soft leather and eyed the bottle of wine chilling in a bucket of ice. She leaned her head back. She almost groaned. Dammit. Lopez was right. She could get used to this, too.

"Wine?"

"Ummm..." She couldn't drink. She couldn't have her senses dulled. Could she? Who would make sure they got to the hotel safely? Who would watch the luggage? She slid her hand along her hip. Shit. Her switchblade wasn't there. The casino they were staying at wouldn't let them carry weapons, so they'd had to leave them back home. Without her knife, she felt naked even in a T-shirt and jeans.

"Take the stick out of your ass." Lopez shoved a semi-full wineglass in her hand. "You're on vacation."

True. She was on vacation. She was going to have fun if it killed her. Shay took a sip. Ick. Heavily sour, light on grape. Where was a beer when she needed one?

Vegas, baby.

CHAPTER TWO

THE LIMO PULLED up to the Pura Vida Hotel and Spa. Shay's sunglasses cut through the glow as she climbed out and stared up at the gleaming tower of glass, the Vegas sun pinging light off the fifty-story wall of windows.

Palm trees lined the sidewalk to the entrance, and a huge sign that undoubtedly glowed with neon after dark stood out front. Pura Vida: A Costa Rican Retreat. The board underneath flashed the messages "Catch the CMAA awards" and "Loosest Slots in Vegas."

The rest of Chicago's Finest piled out of the car as bellhops in white collarless shirts descended, grabbing their luggage and heading back toward the building. Shay followed closely behind her suitcase. Not because she thought it might get stolen, but because the glare from the building temporarily blinded her and all she could see was the back of her red carry-on.

And really, she was always afraid her stuff would

be stolen. She was raised in Chicago, where a five-finger discount was the norm.

She walked through the automatic door and tripped over her luggage. "I'm sorry." She smiled at the bellhop, who looked younger than her brother. Damn sun was in the lobby, too.

"No, no, miss, it's my fault. I shouldn't have stopped, but things are a little chaotic today." The bellhop waited with her for a line to open up at the front desk.

Chaos was an understatement. The huge sign in the foyer didn't have neon, but it screamed in bold red that the Country Music Artist Awards were this week. Apparently, that translated to madhouse.

Sunglass-wearing men and women giggled and flirted while what appeared to be their harried assistants checked in and ensured that there were no red foods in their employer's room giving off negative energy, or some other ridiculous demand. People waiting in line huffed, and others yelled at the bellhop for stacking their luggage in the wrong order.

What she'd signed on for was now becoming abundantly clear. And dammit if she didn't wish she could go wheels up right back to Chicago.

Tomorrow night was going to be interesting. She didn't like interesting. She liked mundane, logical, controlled. When Adam asked her to help guard-slash-assist with the jewelry for the awards, the interacting with celebrities part slipped her radar. She figured she'd guard jewelry—yes—but not that the jewelry would be wrapped around entitled necks. She'd imagined hanging with her friends in Vegas the rest of the time, watching shows, hitting up buffet after buffet, plus the bachelorette party for Adam's fiancée. The glitz and glamour of Sin City would mess up anybody's radar. Had she mentioned the buffets? There was one with a chocolate fountain. Who could concentrate after news like that?

She inched forward.

"*Waa. Waa.*"

A sound came from something at Shay's feet, and sharp little claws brushed against her ankle. Shay jumped and reached for her hip. Damn knife—or lack of knife. She looked down into beady little eyes attached to a furry brown head. Curved dagger claws poked at her leg. "What the hell kind of monkey is that?"

"*Waa. Waa.*" The tiny little Chewbacca-thing with a pink bow stuck to its head leaned against Shay's ankle. The monkey's eyes danced with mischief as it released Shay's leg and hobbled across the floor to a man in a suit. It climbed up his body and curled up in his arms.

A girl in safari-wear whose name tag said SUE glared at Shay. "Davina's not a monkey. She's a two-toed sloth." With a sniff, she turned to look at the long-haired ankle-biter. Sloth. Whatever.

Safari-girl's glower was replaced by a giggle as she watched the hairy beast. Or maybe she was laughing at the gorgeous man holding the little ankle-biter.

Reddish-brown hair. Gorgeous smile. Suit that

hugged his body in all the right places. The man, of course, not the sloth.

The sloth rested her little head on the man's shoulder. Looked comfortable. If Shay were that close, she might have rested her head there, too.

"Davina." Suit guy sighed, but the smile on his face gave him away. He liked the little hairball.

Well, damn. Wasn't that the cutest thing ever? The sloth, of course, not the man.

If her divorce taught her anything, she didn't need nor want a man in her life. Men brought problems, and she had enough of those.

"She can't help it, Doyle." Her nametag might say Sue, but Susie Safari fit her blonde hair and googly-eyed stare better. "You're just irresistible." Susie Safari batted her pretty little blonde lashes as the man walked closer.

Not that Shay was complaining. The closer he got, the better he looked.

He whispered something to Davina, nuzzling her fur. She wrapped her arms around his neck as she stared at him in mammal-love. The hairball had it bad. Davina lurched, reaching for the top of Doyle's head and ripping the earpiece out of his ear. Little troublemaker.

"No, honey. I need to hear my team." He grabbed the bit of plastic before it landed in the critter's mouth. He tried to hand Davina over to Safari Sue, but the furball wasn't having it. She wanted to stay in Doyle's arms, rest her tiny head on his broad shoulders, and look longingly into his eyes.

Sounded like heaven.

Then his eyes met Shay's. Deep green eyes. Gorgeous deep green.

Shay didn't do green eyes, but his were the color of emeralds or Ireland or some sappy crap like that. And no matter how much she wanted to look away, she couldn't make her head turn.

She sounded like the love-struck sloth. Thankfully, she had deniability. She hadn't said any of it out loud. She dragged her eyes away from him. There. Easy. She kept them fixed on the sloth. Much safer.

"Come here, Davina," Susie Safari cooed. "Time to head back to the zoo for lunch." Nothing. The sloth hung onto tall, built, and handsome for dear life. "Food," Suzie sang. The fuzzball's grip loosened, and she practically jumped into Susie's arms.

"It could hurt my ego that she so easily leaves me for food," gorgeous suit-man said as he patted Davina's back.

"I doubt you're suffering." Susie Safari held onto Davina with one hand while trailing a finger down his chest with the other. "Now, if you'd hold me like that, I promise not to hurt your ego."

He sighed. "We had this discussion."

"I know. You won't date coworkers." She spun and walked away.

Surprising. Susie Safari gave the man a blatant screw-me grope, and he turned her down. It wasn't very often a man surprised Shay.

"I'm Garret Doyle." Suit-man held out a hand to Shay. When the hell had he gotten this close to her?

People didn't sneak up on Shay. She kept her head on a swivel. It was part of working the streets as a cop. Yet suit-man showed up, and she became distractible. He was dangerous. She couldn't seem to form coherent thoughts around him. Wait—he just said his first name. What was it?

Garret. He'd said his name was Garret. And he had his hand out. That was normal. As a detective, she'd shaken a lot of hands. This was just like any of those situations. She just had to focus on the mundane and not on the man.

Shay slid her hand in his. See? Mundane.

She looked at their hands joined together. Hers were not dainty like some women. But even so, her dark hand was dwarfed in his long ivory grip. Large. Strong. The warmth of his fingers seeped into every pore like a flare bathing her inside with light.

Smart little sloth, wanting to stay in those arms, with those hands. Shay was surprised the fuzzball left.

What those fingers could do to a woman's body. She could only imagine what those hands must feel like stroking her—

Stop. She pulled away. This was not focusing on the mundane. Epic fail.

"Do you have a name?" full pink lips asked as they arched into a gorgeous smile, showing white teeth.

Gorgeous smile. Dammit. She was always a sucker for a gorgeous smile.

"Do you. Have a name?" he asked again.

What a dumb question. Obviously, she had a name. And she knew it, too. Ummm...

"Washington." Lopez bumped her shoulder. "Wake the fuck up."

She swung toward him, followed his pointing finger to the front desk, where the bellhop stood with her suitcase. Her turn. Dammit. She turned to suit-man... Garret. "Shay Washington."

"Nice to meet you, Shay Washington." He slid his transmitter back into his ear. She watched him walk away. Nummy. Just because she wasn't in the market didn't mean she couldn't do a little window shopping. And she liked this window. A lot. He looked as good going as he did coming.

Maybe not the best phrasing, because now all she could think about was watching the man coming. Was that bad?

He turned and smiled. "Enjoy your stay at Pura Vida." His voice was pure silk, and it licked all the way down her body. Damn.

If he was going to walk around entertaining her eyes, and his voice was going to strum her core like a guitar, she would definitely enjoy her time here.

CHAPTER THREE

GARRET STOOD off to the side of the lobby and watched the throngs of people check-in. Scratch that. He *should* be watching the throngs of people check-in. Instead, he couldn't keep his eyes off Shay Washington.

Everything about her screamed cop. The way her eyes drank in the scene around her. Her no-nonsense demeanor. The fact she didn't flinch when lover boy swore like a sailor. Hell. Even Garret flinched, and he'd been a sailor. His father raised him better. You didn't talk to a woman that way. Which was probably why his parents were happily married and enjoying their golden years back at the family farm in Montana.

He'd noticed her when she first walked in. Black hair. Plump lips. But nothing prepared him for those eyes. Light brown gems set against dark skin. He'd almost dropped Davina after one glance. And then she looked at him. Their eyes locked, and he was lost.

Lost? He didn't get lost. Even when things with his

ex-wife had been good, he'd always had control. He never got lost. Ever.

"Doyle, you're needed in the vault," Sal Ruiz said over the receiver.

Garret moved. Being summoned to the vault by Sal on a good day was a bad thing. With the rash of burglaries going around, it was downright disastrous. "Ten-Four."

Garret turned away from the Shay eye candy and nodded to one of the security officers standing near the wall. "Hold down the fort."

"Do you need help?" the guy asked.

"No. Stay here. I'll call out if you're needed." Garret slid calmly through the crowd in the lobby. No need to cause a scene and break out into a run. Whatever happened, already happened. That didn't mean he wanted to move slow.

He dodged women with Chihuahuas in purses and long blood-red nails and overflowing luggage carts. Whistles and bells welcomed him onto the casino floor as he dodged men in floral shirts carrying glasses of beer. He was used to crazy. Pura Vida had the casino, bars, and swimming pools. Hell, they even had an onsite zoo. The building was where chaos thrived, but this award show was a whole new level, with everyone on high alert.

Garret swiped his key card over the sensor, and the plain door to the tunnels clicked open. With all the prying eyes of the guests gone, Garret opened his stride and ran down the stairs and through the cement halls. The vault was right above the security office, which was in the center of the lowest floor of the building. A veritable fortress underneath the hotel. Between the underground passageways and side halls, his team was five minutes or less away from every point in the hotel if they ran. It was a big hotel.

His steps faltered as he came to the vault room. Loud voices carried into the hallway. He cranked his head side to side, neck crackling, before waving his badge at the sensor and opening the door.

The room was filled with suits. Angry suits. And even though the office that led to the vault was as big as a small-screen movie theatre, it still wasn't big enough.

"What happened?"

The head cashier waved at the broken lock on the outer door. "Someone broke into this room."

"What about the vault?" If someone got into their vault…holy hell. Garret would have to invest in Tums, because his stomach would be in perpetual knots. He stared at the tiny gouges between the door and the body of the vault. "Someone tried to jimmy it open?" That didn't make any sense.

The head cashier shrugged. "I was on the new break schedule, and I ran to the washroom. I locked the vault and the outer door before I left."

They'd decided to stagger breaks, so outsiders wouldn't know when the vault room would be unguarded. But they'd also started locking the vault when not in use. It was a pain to open every time they needed it, but a necessary evil with everything going on.

One of Garret's men, Rick Drakos, stood off to the

side while the managers poked at the door. "So maybe this jewelry bandit didn't know that we started closing the vault."

"Maybe." Garret didn't like it.

Viola Abreau, the hotel manager, pointed at the vault with one manicured finger. "Either way, I have millions of dollars of jewelry and gift bags in there. I have people with money overrunning my hotel. I need to know you have this handled."

Garret nodded. "Yes. It's handled." Like hell it was handled.

"Good. I don't have to tell you how important this weekend is. If we can handle these awards, we are looking at other shows as well—namely the International Jewelry Show. This would put us on the map." Viola straightened to her full height and eyed Garret. "We need this."

They needed it, all right. They were a relatively new hotel. Relatively meant that the newness factor was wearing off and they were building a clientele, but not fast enough. The problem was, you couldn't trip in this town without bumping into a hotel. They needed to find a niche, and they needed it now. Preferably before the investors pulled the plug and sold the building to MGM. And the rumors had already begun.

Then the International Jewelry Show expressed an interest. They were looking for a new residence for the show. Over two thousand vendors, thirty-thousand industry professionals, and who knew how many up-market clientele would come to the hotel. Millions of dollars a year could be guaranteed with that one annual booking.

"Byrnes and Company is on the IJS board. They can make or break us on this."

"I'll personally make sure it goes off without a hitch." Garret was betting his job on those words. But then again, it was Vegas. Where better to wager a bet? And after being in the Navy for ten years, he'd had his share of no-win situations. He'd always come out on top —except the one time. But he didn't think about that anymore.

The manager's nod turned into a shake of her head, making her upswept dark-blonde hair bobble. "I know. It's just..." She sighed. The woman obviously felt the stress as much as Garret. "If we fail, your team is gone. MGM has their own security company."

"And their own management." Which meant Garret and all the management staff would be out of a job. "I know what's at stake."

The manager nodded before she walked out the door, followed by all her little supervisor minions.

Garret would do whatever it took to make sure this award show went off without a problem. He didn't have a choice. It was either that or let everyone down. He'd already done that once. He refused to do it again.

CHAPTER FOUR

THE NEXT DAY, Shay stood behind one of the long tables and asked herself, again, why she was here.

Bright blue silk covered the six hotel folding tables. Each table held two black velvet displays. Sparkly, shiny ridiculousness. More diamonds than an African mine. Not that Byrnes and Company used blood diamonds. She'd done her research. She wouldn't be here if they did. Not even a free trip to Vegas could get her to support that.

Full-length mirrors were scattered around the conference room. Besides her, Perretti, Lopez, and Adam Byrnes all paced the perimeter, making sure the jewelry on display wasn't easy to get to. The plan was for the Chicago cops to stand behind the tables and keep an eye on the celebrities as they perused the diamond library. Adam's fiancée Allison Southby, her sister Brook, and their friends Julie Connelly and Ben Mooring would coddle the country music stars while they decided which necklace would go best with their designer dresses.

"I think I need one more person to help with jewelry tomorrow." Allison batted her lashes at Adam, the owner of Byrnes and Company. His job with the Chicago Police Department made him more of a silent owner because he didn't have time to run the daily operations. Which was where Allison came in. She was the one who set up this jewelry roadshow, the reason they were all here today, providing the already rich and wealthy with borrowed bling for their stroll down the red carpet. She was the one putting Byrnes and Company on the map.

Adam pulled Allison into him, one arm around her back. "Don't look at me. I'm guarding your body."

"I thought you were guarding the jewelry."

He kissed her. "That too."

"Get a room." Brook made a gagging noise. "You've been together for over a year now. Aren't you two past this yet?"

"Amen." Perretti high-fived his woman.

Lopez pointed to Brook and then Perretti. "Wait, didn't her tongue get lost in your mouth on the plane ride here? I thought she'd never be able to experience the joy of a lollypop again." He grinned like a shark. "But at least your tonsils are all clean now."

Perretti glared. "Shut it, Lopez."

"Whatever, tonsil-hockey."

"Jealous?" Perretti placed his lips on Brook's. A long, unnecessary attempt to win the testosterone-fueled game.

Lopez rolled his eyes. "Not even close, tonsil-hockey. I'm seeing the redhead tonight. All aboard for a ride on the friendly thighs."

"Pig." Allison threw a velvet board at Lopez at the same time a cell phone hit his head with a thud.

"Ow." He snatched the phone from the floor. "Thanks, I needed a new phone."

Perretti pulled away from Brook and shook his head. He leaned down, picking up the velvet board and handing it back to Allison.

Shay held out her hand for the phone that had—somehow—flown from her hand. "Give it back."

"But you gave it to me. To my head, to be exact." Lopez played with the screen, obviously trying to break her passcode.

Shay didn't move, just kept her hand in Lopez's face. "It slipped." And it had. In her defense, Lopez was being an idiot. And the phone just sort of flew toward his thick head. Some kind of magnetic attraction.

"Fine." He dropped it in her hand. "It's not the latest version anyway."

"Excuse me?" Garret stood in the doorway all sexy and fine—looking all professional with his clipboard, long fingers wrapped around a pen. He couldn't have been standing there long, but apparently long enough to have a smirk on his face. "First of all, there's a delivery at the dock. Big boxes."

"Oh, it's probably the jewelry for the gift bags." Allison bounced up and down, pointing at the men in the room. "You three come with me."

"I'm going too. I want to see." Brook wasn't exactly a jewelry girl, but she was even less a stuck-in-one-room-for-hours girl. Shay could understand.

"Do you need directions?" Garret marked off something on his clipboard. The smirk disappeared, replaced by a faint frown.

"Nope, I remember from yesterday." Allison had arrived early with Adam and had apparently gotten a pretty good lay of the land because she disappeared, taking everyone with her.

Garret worked a few pages loose and held them out. "Second, I need someone to go over these."

Shay was the only one left in the room. How did that happen? Better yet, why did that happen? She should not be left alone with this man. It was like putting a crackhead in front of a big pile of powder and saying, "don't touch". They always touched.

And Shay did not want to touch. She sighed. "Go over what?" She was definitely the crackhead in this scenario.

He set the small stack of paper on a table and pushed a lamp aside. Apparently, bling needed lots of light to show off the sparkle because each table had a mirror and lamp for that purpose.

Shay checked out the pages. There were names. Her name, everyone from Chicago PD, and her friends from the jewelry company.

"So, I take it you're Chicago PD like Adam and Joe." Garret leaned over, inches from her face.

Good gracious, he smelled amazing. Spiced eucalyptus. "I'm Joe's partner."

"Really? So, you're a detective." His eyebrow curved up. Was it shock? Awe? Who knew.

"Yep." Well, she was up until yesterday. Not that she was going into specifics about her promotion with him.

"Hmmm..." That hum didn't sound like awe. That left shock.

"What hmm?" Was it so unbelievable that she'd made detective?

"Yeah, you act like a detective, but you don't really look like one."

She didn't look like a detective? Gee, was it the color of her skin, or her vagina? Over the years, she'd met both kinds, racists and sexists. Neither kind could imagine she'd been a cop—let alone detective, sergeant, and now lieutenant. They'd probably flip their crap if they knew about the last one. Thankfully, for every racist or sexist, there was a decent person who didn't care about skin color or what body parts she had. They just wanted the best person for the job. Out of curiosity, she asked, "What does a detective look like?"

He smiled. His eyes sparkled as he looked up at her. "Uglier."

Shay laughed. That wasn't exactly what she expected. "I won't tell Adam and Joe you said that. It might hurt their feelings."

"I've spent the past few days with Adam. If Joe is anything like him, nothing can penetrate those egos."

"I've spent the past few years with Joe, and no, nothing gets through that ego."

He smiled that gorgeous smile. Some women liked

abs, some liked a pretty face. Shay was all about the smile—not that Garret didn't have a stellar body and attractive face.

He wasn't bad to look at. But once he smiled? Good heavens. It took everything she had not to melt into a huge pile of drool. She ran a hand over her mouth. Was she drooling?

Garret tapped the top page. "This is the list of approved volunteers. Can you take a look at it? Your entire team, with names and phone numbers, should be on this list." He fanned the pages with one hand, while the other rested briefly on her back. The way you'd do with a coworker. The heat of him shouldn't have made her skin tingle. The way his hand fit perfectly along the curve of her spine shouldn't make her want to lean back and soak him in.

"If Byrnes and Company have added anyone, I need that information," Garret said. "This is the bible. My guys won't let anyone in unless they're on this list. Got it?"

She couldn't hear anything over the fireworks going off in her head. Those fingers were magic. "Yep." She'd dealt with good-looking men before. She could totally handle this. She glanced over the names and numbers. She recognized a few of them. The ones of her coworkers and her friends. She verified her own number. It all looked good. "We're all here."

"Are you sure?" he asked, like he doubted her.

"Yes." She handed him the pages, but he wouldn't take them.

"Could you just double-check? This is important.

We won't have time to deal with issues during the event."

She checked over the names again. "Still all there."

"I just need you to take this seriously."

What was his problem? There were a few things in life Shay could be accused of—not taking things seriously was not one of them. She was always serious. Someone had to be. "Would you like me to highlight the names or circle them to show I've taken my job seriously? Take a blood oath?"

"Fine." He pointed to a number at the top of the list. "There's my phone number if you need me."

She pulled out her phone and typed it in. For work purposes. It's not like she wanted his number.

"Otherwise, Sal Ruiz will be in the room with you the entire time."

The entire time? That seemed like overkill. She handed over the list and slid her phone in her pocket. "We have four cops. We should be all right if he's needed somewhere else."

"Nope. He's all yours." He hesitated. "I need to confirm that none of you brought a gun. The casino rules apply to everybody—no outside weapons. No matter who you are."

"No one brought a gun." Although it physically hurt Shay to be without one.

"Good. Let me introduce you to Sal Ruiz. Hey, Sal," he called to a man down the hall, and the guy lumbered toward them.

Lumbered was a good word for it. He was a mountain. About six feet tall, bald, bulked up arms and legs.

The kind of guy you didn't want to mess with because he could snap the average person in half. The kind of guy you wanted guarding the family jewels. Or Byrnes and Company's jewels, anyway.

"Salvador Ruiz, this is Detective Shay Washington. She'll be in the room with you tomorrow."

"Nice, always good to have another cop on hand." Sal shook her hand. "Especially with the rash of jewelry burglaries going on—"

"Burglaries?" Shay hadn't heard about any burglaries. "Does Byrnes know about this?"

"It's nothing that needs to concern you." Garret glared at Sal.

Wait, what exactly did that mean? It sounded like no one from her team had been informed and that Garrett had no intention of telling them. "A rash of jewelry burglaries doesn't concern me? Us? We'll have millions of dollars of jewelry sitting in this room. We need to be aware of all the threats." Shay's pulse raced. What else weren't they being told?

"There's nothing to worry about." Garret's tone gentled and slowed—in other words, he was patronizing her. "If it was an issue we would have brought it up earlier. There have been a few burglaries at some of the other hotels, and jewelry was stolen. But it's nothing that concerns us."

Every word was a knife to Shay's patience. Every look that Garret and Sal shared tickled the back of her collar. She ran a hand over the back of her neck as her skin prickled. "But..." Shay said, and was waved off by Garret.

He. Waved. Her. Off. She wanted to slip him into an arm bar and slam his teeth into the wall.

"We have things under control here." Garret pulled out his cell phone and ran his finger over the screen. Apparently, he was done with her questions. He looked so cute. Too bad he opened his arrogant mouth and ruined it.

Too bad her questions weren't done with him. "So, is there anything else you've been hiding about this job?"

"Hiding?" Garret's eyes left his phone. "We're not hiding anything. I could use my own staff, but I *allowed* Byrnes and Company to bring their own security. If that decision threatens my building or our security in any way, I will pull the plug."

"So do my questions threaten your security? Or does it merely threaten your manhood?" A hand touched her elbow. She was about to shake it off, but the gentle pull came from Sal.

His smile was forced, but the concern in his eyes seemed real. "Detective, I would love to show you around, let you see the space we're working with." Sal dropped his hand and motioned toward a door at the back of the hall.

Good idea. Talking to Pura Vida's arrogant dictator was not getting her anything—except a potential ulcer. She followed Sal out the door into another big room with doors at either end. A red carpet stretched from one set of doors to the other. Across from her, a black banner with the CMAA logo splashed across an expanse of white wall.

Sal headed for one set of doors. "This area is closed off to everyone but security and awards staff until the celebrities start walking the red carpet tomorrow night. The door we just came through will be locked, so no one can get back to the jewelry room." Sal swiped a key card and held the door for her. Beyond that was a manned desk. The attendant nodded at them as they passed, and Sal led Shay down a hallway into a big atrium. Staff was setting up inconspicuous metal detectors.

"No guns or weapons are allowed past this point." He paused outside another door. "This is the main entrance to the jewelry room. We'll have one of our guys and one of your guys posted here to let everybody on the list through."

Shay knew from wandering the hotel that this side of Pura Vida was conference rooms and the zoo entrance. The dinging of the casino felt like it was in another world. Yeah, this was a good post. She'd get to guard the door and not deal with jewelry. "I can monitor the door."

"Sure." Sal smiled and slid his keycard through the door reader. With a click, they were inside the jewelry room again.

The quiet jewelry room had once again been taken over by her coworkers. Garret leaned against one of the tables checking items off of a list on his clipboard, and everyone else bounced around the room, opening boxes and tagging jewelry.

Except for Lopez. He was staring at his phone, but

that didn't stop his mouth from moving. "Where the hell you been?" he asked.

"Recon. I'm going to work the door." Shay smiled. The idea was sounding better and better.

"No." Such a short time, and she not only knew Garrett's voice, it actually made her cringe. And then the word he'd said actually registered. He'd told her no.

"No?"

"I've asked Lopez to work the door. You'll be in here."

Lopez? The womanizing man-whore? The women wouldn't get in the front door, because he'd be too busy trying to stick his, his...tongue down their throats.

"Excuse me?" And anyway, who the hell was he to tell her where to go? She worked with Byrnes, not him. Garret didn't have any right to tell her what to do. The anger that had been building since he'd opened his mouth this morning zipped through her veins, making her jumpy. He had no right. "Who the hell are—"

"I really need you inside." Allison smiled and rested a hand on her arm.

"Fine." Shay hated giving that man his way, but she'd do anything for her friends.

Garrett smirked from the other side of the room. "Lopez, I'll take you to meet the guy you'll be working with tomorrow."

"Jackass." Shay was sure she'd said that under her breath. But if she had, then Sal must have inched closer without her knowing, because all of a sudden he was on her six.

"He can be, but he's serious. If he thinks his

building isn't secure with you here, he'll pull you from the rotation."

"Why wouldn't the building be secure?" Were they back to this? Why would she be a threat to the security of the building? Because she was black? A woman? She'd like to think that people were more evolved than that. But she'd had to play the prove-your-worth game too many times over the years. She knew the signs.

Garret might be fun to look at and have incredible sloth-side manners, maybe because he was a sloth-like human. No, that was being too cruel to sloths. The fuzzy beast seemed decent compared to Garret. Apparently, he had no respect for women, or maybe it was just that he had no respect for her. Either way, Shay wasn't the type to put up with that from anyone.

CHAPTER FIVE

A FEW HOURS LATER, Garret leaned against a table out in the hall and watched Shay set up with her team through the propped open door. He might have been a bit of dick about the whole burglaries thing and the posting at the door. The icy stare she threw his way said he might have been slightly more than a bit. However, he'd be working that main hall tomorrow night, and he'd never get a thing done if she was there—standing in the doorway, not realizing how incredibly hot she really was.

Okay. He was a grownup, he would have gotten it done, but why torture himself?

"Garret, how are things going?" Viola approached the hall table and looked in the jewelry room.

"On target. We've ramped up security in the vault and surrounding this room." Garret nodded to the main door. "We have one of the Chicago cops and Sal on the inner door, and I'll be at the outer door with one of the Chicago cops and two of my guys."

Viola shook her head. "I want you as close to this room as possible."

Having him at the outer door—the first line of defense and nowhere near Shay—was definitely the better option. "I think that we'll be better served if I'm at the outer door. I'll move one of the other guys over here."

"Garret, you know I don't normally interfere with security, but I need this. I would feel better if you were at the door here. If anyone tries to leave with a piece of jewelry, you'll be right there to stop them."

Viola was right. She never got in the way of Garret and his team. And the fact that she was making this request meant she needed him to follow through. "If it would make you feel better."

"Thank you." She smiled. "I'm going to go check on the food. Last I heard, they didn't have enough chicken."

"Chicken? How do you run out of chicken?" Especially since they had an onsite buffet, plus mountains of food sitting in fridges back there.

"No clue. It's like running out of salt or something." She shook her head. "If I live through this award show, it will be a miracle."

"And you want to bring more shows onsite."

"I should have my head examined." She smiled and walked out the door.

Inside the room, Shay leaned over and pushed a table. She poked her tongue out as she slid the legs along the carpet. Her collared shirt only had three buttons undone, but Garret was transfixed by a glimpse of soft dark cleavage, leading his imagination on a journey. Her body wasn't rail-thin. It was soft and perfect. When she laughed, even the jiggle of her chest couldn't distract him from the gorgeous smile lighting up her face.

Eight hours of looking at that smile.

Eight hours of being less than a foot away.

After this, *he* was going to need his head examined.

"So..." Sal leaned against the table next to Garret.

"So." Garret refocused on the paperwork in his hands. He needed to redo the schedule and get the changes out to his crew. Sal's breath hung in Garret's ear. The man obviously had something to tell him, but instead of just saying it, he breathed, loudly, in Garret's personal space. "Do you have something to say, Sal? If so, get it over with."

"I was giving you a chance to yell. I'm assuming you're pissed I told Shay about the burglaries."

Yeah, Sal did do that, didn't he? Garret should be pissed, but somehow he wasn't. "You couldn't know." He headed toward the steps leading to the Bunker. A headache crawled up his neck and was moments away from latching onto his head. Might as well be proactive, medicate before the throbbing started.

"Couldn't know what? That you were hiding that piece of information?"

Et tu? Garret swiped his badge and flipped open the Bunker door, walking straight through to his office. *Brute* followed. "I wasn't hiding it," Garret admitted. He just wasn't as forthcoming as he could have been.

"They should've been told. They're jewelry heists. They're carrying at least a half-million in jewels."

"They weren't jewelry heists. They were heists that included jewels."

"And there's a difference?"

"Intent." Garret threw his paperwork on his clutter-free desk. He took off his jacket and hung it on the back of his door. Everything had a place in his office, and everything was in that place. When things got out of control, other things went south.

Garret didn't like south. He didn't like having people in his business, in his hotel. Especially gorgeous detectives that were smart as a whip and lashed at his patience.

Fact was, she had every right to know what had happened. She had every right to know about the jewel thief and their penchant for sparkly diamonds. But she had no right to question his control of the situation.

"Hey, boss." Mary walked into his office and brushed past Sal, whose tongue was hanging out of his mouth. His infatuation was a sexual harassment suit waiting to happen.

Fortunately, she seemed to like him too. Unfortunately, they both learned how to talk to the opposite sex in kindergarten.

"Hi to you too, Mary." Sal grabbed at the file in her hands.

She yanked back before he could pull it away. "This is above your pay grade, Sal."

"I could double-check your reports, you know, help you with all the big words." Sal leaned over as Mary slid the file in front of Garret. They had the verbal shoving match perfected, now all they needed was to pass a note back and forth. *Do you like me? Check yes or no.*

"Did you secure that situation on the floor?" Garret opened the file and sifted through the write-ups. While he handled the CMAA setup, Mary was running the floor. With the exception of Sal, there wasn't anyone he trusted more.

Mary ran a hand through her short light-brown hair and turned back to Garret. "Yeah, which one? We had a pickpocket in the high roller room and a fight at the penny slots. The little shits put up a crazy fight. Las Vegas PD picked them all up." She smoothed the collar of her pantsuit and gave him a little wave. "I'm out of here."

"Get some rest," Garret told her. "Tomorrow will be a nightmare."

Sal followed Mary out the door, and Garret tried to concentrate on the reports. The room was quiet. Too quiet. He switched the screen in his office to the camera in the jewelry room.

Shay sat at the table, looking so out of place. So bored. Her place wasn't behind a desk; she obviously belonged on the beat, chasing leads or whatever she did back in Chicago.

Chicago. After the CMAAs, she'd go back home, and he'd be here. Alone.

Been there. Wore the shirt. Two years ago, his wife had walked away. Maybe it wouldn't have hurt so much if she'd looked back, been remorseful, maybe pretended to care. But she hadn't. She'd run back to Montana like she was being chased by scorpions.

He wasn't doing this again. He wasn't falling for someone who'd run. Who wouldn't turn back and look at him. Wouldn't miss him at all. No matter how full her lips or how deep her eyes.

Crap.

He turned off the monitor. He wasn't doing this again. He just had to keep reminding himself.

CHAPTER SIX

SHAY'S first full day of vacation in Vegas didn't include buffets or slot machines. They'd sat in a back room, all hands on deck, tagging jewelry and logging the names of the celebrities who would be stopping by tomorrow.

So much better than unlimited crab legs. *Not.*

She checked her watch. Eight p.m. She could finally hit one of those crab-troughs since all the jewelry was tagged, sorted, and resting comfortably in the hotel vault.

The rest of the women had all left, taking the girly giggles and gossip up to the suite she was sharing with Allison, Brook, and Julie. Shay stood, making sure her phone was in her pocket. She could play a few games on it while she ate her weight in shellfish.

"Shay, we need you." Joe popped his head around the corner. Disappointment bubbled in Shay's chest as she walked to the table in the center of the hall, visions of crab legs being trampled by a Godzilla-sized Joe running through her head.

Joe, Adam, and the jerk who ran the hotel security leaned over the center, pointing and grunting.

Adam looked up from the table. "Where's Lopez?"

"Stewardess," Joe and Shay said at the same time. Like that was all that needed to be said and everyone got it. Apparently, that *was* all that needed to be said, as everyone turned their attention back to the floor plans on the table.

Garret pointed at the jewelry room on the map. "So the cameras cover every inch around this room."

Shay leaned over the table. The layout they had here was impressive, as well as the size. And the fact that the jerk managed to keep the location locked down almost left her in awe. Almost. She wasn't a big fan of sexist pigs.

"Do we get to see the camera room?" Adam's attention never left the table, but he couldn't hide his excitement. He was like Gran in the bingo hall, complete with wide eyes and lust.

Garret nodded. "Yeah, I think we can arrange that. Follow me."

Shay followed the men out of the room and along a brightly lit hallway to a heavy metal door. After a beep from Garret's key card, they took the cement stairs down to another hallway.

Bulbs in the ceiling gave off dreary yellow light. The soggy smell hung in the air as they walked farther and farther down more dark stairs and through hallways into the bowels of the hotel.

They walked another couple of minutes in silence. Every once in a while, Joe would ask about a camera or about the security procedures, or they'd pass someone Garret knew, but overall it was dark and chilly.

Garret used his magic card on a red metal door, and opened it to the soft hum of electronics and voices. A woman and a man sat behind a huge desk filled with dials, buttons and keys, and stared at one of the screens on the wall. Another guy stood off to the side.

Shay should be shocked there was a woman on Garret's security team, but she couldn't get over the screens. Twenty of them. It was like NASA meets Buffalo Wild Wings. One large screen sat in the center, with little screens around it.

Even one of the little screens was bigger than her computer back at CPD, twenty-two inches at least.

"Shit. Run it again," the woman said.

The video on the largest screen slowed to a frame-by-frame of one of the tables in the casino. A guy sitting at the table touched the chips in front of the woman sitting next to him and brought his arm back. It was like he was tapping her chips for luck and went back to his hand.

"What's he up to?" the guy at the controls asked. The controls cast an eerie blue glow over his white complexion.

Garrett waited till they were all in the room before closing the door. "What's going on, Bentley?"

The woman shook her head. Her long black hair was tied up in the back, showing dark russet-brown skin. She moved her ring-laden left hand to the screen. "This creep is up to something, but I can't see what."

"We've been watching him for a few minutes, and he just taps her chips and backs off," the guy standing by the wall added.

Garret came up behind the desk. "Start it from the beginning."

Adam and Joe moved closer. Shay stood back and watched the guy on the screen put his fingers near the woman next to him and pull back. He played a hand, and then looked over at another table. His eyes darted back and forth. Then he inched toward the woman next to him.

And stopped. Again.

What was he up to? The guy played another hand. Inched toward his neighbor, not the same woman as before. So, it wasn't her...

Wait. It wasn't her. And his eyes—

"Hold on. Back up." Shay walked up to the screen. "Watch this. Eyes left, right, left, right. And then he leans into the woman on his left." Shay pointed off the screen to the right. "Okay, here we go again. Eyes left, right, left, right. Back to the woman on his left. What's to the right of this table?"

"More tables." The woman Garret had called Bentley smiled, and eyed the small screens. "Pull up thirty-seven," she told the guy working the controls.

The big screen switched to another camera, another table with a brunette shaking her hair. The men at the table were barely keeping the drool under control. Her eyes roamed to the left. As the guy at the table played at taking the chips from his neighbor, she wound her hand around the top of her neighbor's stack and slid it into her pocket.

"A diversion." Garret smiled as he looked over to Shay.

"That's my partner." Joe slapped her on the back. Hard. She almost fell forward, but managed to keep her feet planted. His smile turned down at the edges. "Well, was my partner."

Yep, that was it. The ache in her chest pulsed. She wasn't going to have Joe around anymore. Or Adam. The guys. Her friends. It was a promotion. She just had to keep remembering that.

Adam started to frown and then smiled. "Why do they need you with her around?"

"I've been trying to figure that out for years." Joe leaned in, the pain in his eyes gone as he smirked. "Don't tell anyone, though. I don't want the zebras to figure that out."

"Zebra?" Sal walked in the room as Bentley and the guy not manning the controls walked out, presumably to apprehend Bonnie and Clyde.

"Sergeant. Lieutenant. Zebra." Joe shrugged. "You know, an ass with stripes."

"I'm sure you don't mean me." Shay shook her head. This is what she'd miss. These guys knew how to keep things light. How to make her smile. When she'd been a beat cop, she'd complained about the zebras that ran CPD. Bitching about management was one of the few perks of the job. Then she'd become an ass with stripes. Not that she regretted her promotions. She'd worked hard for it, and if she played her cards right, she'd be chief in the next ten years.

"Not you Lieutenant." Joe mock-saluted with annoying flair.

Garret looked at Shay. "You're a lieutenant." There was no surprise this time, maybe a little awe.

"Yes." She couldn't help but keep her stare locked on him. He was so gorgeous. Nothing she'd ever fall for, but...who cared about falling? She just wanted to look at the guy. Especially when he looked at her like this. His eyes glowed. Actually glowed. What did that even mean?

Joe cleared his throat. Broke the spell. Her eyes peeled away from the strong muscles and that smile. *Grrr.*

Joe and Adam smirked. Joe met her eyes, and his lips pulled high and wide across his goofy Italian face.

She rolled her eyes. "Shut up."

"Sorry, Washington, I don't believe I said anything."

"Well, Perretti, you don't have to." It was the danger of being partners—wordless understanding. Would she find that in forensics?

Adam looked at his watch. "Joe, we should head up."

"Yep." Joe reached out and shook Garret's hand. "Thanks for giving us a tour. This was—uh—interesting." Joe looked at Shay as he said the word interesting.

Interesting?

Jackass.

Adam followed with a handshake, left out the

commentary and the looking. Adam was turning into her favorite coworker.

"Yes, thank you for the tour." Shay didn't want to shake Garret's hand, but it was common courtesy. And if she didn't, Lord Almighty, she'd never hear the end of it. She wrapped her hand around his.

His hands were everything she remembered. They were immense, smooth, but strong. That one shake told her so much. It told her she wanted to feel those smooth hands running up and down her body. It told her she wanted those strong hands to lift her to the wall as he pressed her against it. It told her she needed to run, run long and fast before she did something she'd regret—or worse, enjoy.

She pulled away after what felt like a second, but the grin on Joe's face said it was longer than that. Son of a bitch. She turned to Sal and shook his hand, keeping her hand in his for a touch too long. That would throw the men off the trail. At least, that was the theory.

Garret's brows curved together. "Do you remember how to get back?"

"I'll see them out." Sal escorted them back to where they started. "See you tomorrow," he said, and left them in the hallway with the red carpet as he headed back down the stairs to the security bunker.

"So, Garret, huh?" Joe nodded as she walked toward the elevators that would take her far away from the questions.

"No Garret, huh."

"He's not a bad-looking guy." Adam hit the button

on the elevator. "He's no me, but not many men are, and I'm taken."

"I'm sure the rest of us will manage to survive even after you're married."

A ding rang out across the hall, and an elevator car slipped open. Adam and Joe walked in. Shay wanted to wait for the next one, but she could see Adam was holding the button to keep the door open. They'd never just let her ride alone in glorious silence. Not when they were having so much fun.

"I think you'll survive with Garret by your side." Joe laughed. Shay almost thought he was going to start doing a kissy-face.

"Please get whatever this is" —Shay waved her hands as she stepped inside— "out of your system. I would hate to get arrested in Las Vegas for beating the ever-loving shit out of you both."

Joe laughed. "Try explaining that one to the captain."

"I'd rather not. So let's just be done with all your little bubblegum antics."

"Bubblegum antics?" Joe turned to Adam. "What are bubblegum antics? Is there actual bubblegum involved? Or only antics?"

"I don't know, but they sound like fun."

The doors slid open at Shay's floor. Thank goodness. She'd had all the *fun* she could possibly have with them. "See you tomorrow."

Male laughter echoed from the elevator as the door closed. She walked down the hall. And now that the hyenas were enclosed in the metal box heading up to their room, not one sound surrounded her.

Not one sound from the hall. Silence was golden, and she was going to embrace it with all she had. Because tomorrow—tomorrow she had a feeling would be loud and crazy.

CHAPTER SEVEN

THE NEXT DAY, Shay couldn't hold back her cringe when Julie cried, "Oh my God, do you know who that is?"

From her post outside the door, Shay angled her head around the doorjamb to watch Julie jump, knocking a cup of water onto her black pantsuit. Julie swore. Wet dripped down the tablecloth onto the floor.

Shay pinched the inside of her wrist so she wouldn't laugh. She was like those British Guard guys, stoic and unmoving. At least, that was the plan. But watching Julie drool over some handsome country star was pretty damn hilarious.

Shay had watched the guy walk in and hadn't reacted—British Guard and all—but she wasn't dead or blind. He was good looking. Dark hair. Dark eyes. His skin touched with a hint of sun. Overall, he was nice to look at. So was the size-zero blonde hanging from his arm.

Small perky nose, smoky eyes, and long blonde hair

teased into a helmet on her head. Good heavens. Shay thought about the teeny album covers on her iPod country music playlist. She knew that face from one of them.

Tall dark and country turned his attention to an old, important-looking man, and blondie took the opportunity to run her hand down Garret's chest. He smiled as she slipped an arm around his waist. Of course he smiled. The woman was gorgeous, and hanging all over him.

What the hell was with Garret, anyway? First the sloth got all starry-eyed, now a Grammy-nominated singer was hanging on him like a koala in a eucalyptus tree. It was like he had a gift for reducing everyone and everything to clingy mammals. Well, maybe not everyone.

Country star dude hadn't drunk the Kool-Aid. In fact, he was glaring laser beams into Garret as he grabbed the blonde's hand and drew her into the jewelry room. Garret's powers only seemed to translate to the female population. Not all that shocking.

Thank goodness Shay was immune. She didn't do that blatant flirt or moony look. Not in real life anyway. Her very vivid and very erotic dream last night didn't count.

Garret's eyes found Shay. He smiled. All white teeth. The room actually heated up a few degrees from the brilliance of that smile. The way he ran those teeth along the inside of her thigh in—what would now be referred to as dreamtopia—pulsed through her mind. Causing other parts of her body to pulse. Dammit.

Dear Lord, please make me stop. She went back to British Guard mode and turned off the dream reel playing on a loop in her mind. Easy. Peasy.

Immune.

She had to be immune. This man was drama with a capital tragedy. And she had enough of that in her life. What she needed was stability, not a tornado of a man knocking around her already crazy life.

Garret walked over and nodded to the muscled security guard on the other side of the doorway. "You can take your break."

Muscles nodded, and Garret took his post. Shay kept her eyes forward. The bulk of the celebrities had been through earlier in the afternoon, so there wasn't much to look at. But if she focused on the one spot on the wall, she wouldn't be tempted to look at Garret.

Not that she didn't want to look. Looking was nice. But if she looked, he might think that was an invitation to talk. Talking was not nice. Although, he'd been nice last night in the security office. For all she knew, that had been temporary insanity.

In the light of day, he'd probably find something stupid to say and ruin their current truce.

"How's it going?" Garret's eyes were on Shay.

She knew this because her eyes had moved to him. Stupid eyes. They needed a lesson in British Guard. "Good." Keep it simple.

Garret moved closer, standing in the doorway, leaning against her jamb. Her jamb! His face was inches away. The mint of his toothpaste made her want to affix herself to his mouth and take a lick. Ugh.

That sounded like something her gran would say. Gran had been harping on Shay to find a nice guy and settle down—or at the minimum find a guy and get down. But Shay never had time. Between raising her brother Shawn and making sure Gran didn't sneak off to the racetrack and lose all her money, Shay's personal life had been a heaping of responsibilities. Not that she minded. She loved her family.

Although all that was coming to end. With Shawn leaving Illinois to study at NYU and her gran spending more and more time out with her boyfriend, Shay was going to be alone. Her family gone.

Garret leaned his shoulder against hers. "That was really impressive last night."

Last night? She tried to remember last night. There was the dream. That dream. Heat crawled up her neck until she remembered, he wasn't there. The heat receded. "Last night?"

"The woman palming chips. You saw the situation before we moved to the other camera."

"I just suggested another camera."

"Don't sell yourself short. It's something I'm always trying to teach my staff. You not only have to see what's right in front of you, but what's not." He bumped her shoulder, and a rush of energy flowed to her core—from having him so close or the sweet things he was saying, she wasn't sure. "It's a great skill to have. Especially as a cop. I can see how you became lieutenant."

"Thanks." All that receded heat was clawing to get back on her face. Even her dark skin wouldn't hide it. She was sure she looked as bright as the whirling cherries on a patrol car. She needed a change of topic. "So, how is everything with the award show going?"

"So far, so good. We've had a few drunk and disorderlies, a few fights. Nothing we didn't expect. And nothing we don't expect to get worse as the night progresses and more alcohol than food gets consumed."

"This whole setup is rather impressive." Shay might have thought this hotel and his security team was remarkable earlier, but he'd been such a jerk, she hadn't wanted to inflate his ego. But something was different. His ego didn't seem to be driving the bus tonight. It was nice. "The security integration is amazing given the massive grounds you have to cover."

"Thanks." His smile practically glowed with pride. But not in a gloating way. It was cute. "It's taken some time to get things in order, but we've got it down now. When we opened, nothing worked. The cameras were glitchy and the turnover was ridiculous. But we've made it work. Sal and Mary stuck with me as we built the department into what it is today."

"I don't think I've met Mary."

"She's amazing. Badass."

Something that definitely wasn't jealousy swirled in Shay's blood, and she curled her hand into a fist. But it wasn't jealousy. That would be ludicrous.

"I think you'd like her. Sal won't admit it, but he's in love with her."

"And you?"

"I'll admit Sal's in love with her." Garret laughed. "I think she likes him, too, but they're both so stubborn, the other may never know."

Shay's laugh bubbled in her chest. So much for British Guard. But it was always ridiculous to her that people weren't honest with the ones they loved.

"I can take over." Muscles was back already. Had it been fifteen minutes?

"Great." Garret pulled away from Shay, taking his warm shoulder and nice words with him. "We should be done in a few minutes. It's died down, and you only have a few people who haven't picked up their jewelry."

"Okay." She watched him walk into the jewelry room. It had been nice talking to him. Who would have thought?

DONE. Twenty minutes later, Shay closed the door to the room as everyone cleaned up. Thank goodness. At one point, they'd had probably thirty people packed into this room. It had been hot and loud. Even standing by the door hadn't help curb the noise.

But now there was silence. No more voices. No more whining. Just lots and lots of glorious silence. Maybe she'd head upstairs, lock the bathroom door and take a bath. She deserved a warm soak after today.

"We're missing one," Allison announced, frowning at a stack of jewelry cases.

Crap. Which meant the night still hadn't ended. She couldn't leave, not without everything locked away in the safe. The hotel security team had moved on to the clubs, where parties had already started raging. That left the CPD to finish up here.

"One more what?" Lopez leaned against the wall. He was staring at the door, probably willing it to open. Shay would put money on him jonesing to head over to Marimba, also known as the club where the young and horny went to dance, and get in there for an hour or so—or in one of the hot country starlets for the night. Either way, he wanted out, and he was getting crabby.

"We loaned sixty-seven pieces," Allison said. "We should have forty-four left. I counted forty-three."

A key jiggled in the lock and Garret's head peeked around the door. "How are things going here? About ready to lock down the leftovers in the safe?"

"We're missing one of the necklaces," Allison told him.

"Wait." Brook reached under a table and came up with a box. "I forgot. I put this down here earlier, during the rush."

"Thank Christ." Lopez stepped away from the wall. "Doyle, can I get tickets to Marimba?"

"Tonight?" Garret laughed, actually laughed, at Lopez. Shay couldn't really blame him. She could only imagine what a cluster that club was tonight.

"Hell, I'll settle for a ticket to Irazú." That was the top-level club—older and more mature, in theory.

From what Shay had heard, it was expensive and gorgeous. With the high-class clientele floating around tonight, settling wouldn't include Irazú.

"We have lines outside the main doors. We're turning people away. Right now, there's at least a five-hour wait, and no one's leaving. I hate to say it, but I don't think anyone will be getting in the clubs unless they're famous."

"Come on, man, you got room for one more," Lopez begged.

"Sorry, but we have to answer to the firefighters. They got codes."

"Damn hose draggers." Lopez actually seemed pissed as he pulled out his phone. His fingers flew across the screen. Shay saw a redheaded flight attendant in his future. "Are we done here?" He kept typing.

"Yeah, I'll take it from here." Adam opened one of the big rolling trunks. "Joe, why don't you and Ben and everybody else head back to the room, and I'll escort the jewelry back to the safe."

"Okay." Joe and Ben walked to the door and waited for Allison, Brook, and Julie to gather sweaters and purses and the multitudes of things that had accumulated over the day. "You coming, Washington?" Joe grumbled.

"I'm going to help Adam out here." Shay opened another trunk and started stacking empty cases inside.

Arms overflowing, everybody else disappeared, leaving Shay and Adam to finished loading the trunks. It shouldn't have been that hard to pack a bunch of empty boxes, but that was part of the problem. Adam wanted all the empties in two trunks, and all the leftover jewelry in one, to make it easier when the jewelry was returned. It was like a game of Tetris, only not fun.

"Ready?" Garret held open the door as Adam rolled the cart holding all three trunks into the hall. They made their way out the door and away from the red carpet. The vault was one floor down from the main floor, right above the NASA-inspired camera room. She followed Garret onto the elevator, pushing the cart against the back wall of the cab. Shay slid around the cart, and Garret moved in next to her. Adam walked in last, turning to watch the closing doors.

The doors dinged as they closed. And then she was in a small metal box with Garret. Not really alone, Adam was there, but he wasn't turning around. He wasn't making a sound. All Shay could see was Garret's broad shoulders in a black suit. All she could smell was Garret's cologne. Sandalwood and spiced eucalyptus.

She'd noticed it earlier, but she was too busy waiting for the shoe to slide into Garret's mouth to focus on his scent. But he hadn't put his foot or any other body part in his mouth. He'd been kind and sweet. Which meant she was able to enjoy the scent without wanting to pummel him.

He smelled good enough to devour. She leaned closer—just a touch closer—breathing him in deeper and deeper. Her body pulsed with every breath. She leaned sideways, and okay, she might not have really been on the verge of falling over, but damn if it didn't feel that way.

Her emotions usually consisted of frustration and anger, with a laugh mixed in now and again. Emotions weren't welcome when you were a woman in a male-dominated profession. Not just that. A Black woman in a white-male-dominated profession. When a woman emoted, they were seen as weak—crazy. And she was the furthest thing from weak. She wasn't going to even touch the whole crazy thing, but if anyone asked her ex-husband— Then again, who cared what he thought.

But Garret made her want to care. He made her uneasy and off-balance. Discomfort and imbalance would be the death of her, figuratively anyway, since she was on vacation. And wasn't this the time to be off her game, when the most strenuous thing she needed to do was sip margaritas by the pool?

The doors dinged again, and the jewels were on their way. She pushed. Adam pulled. Garret led the way down the hall and through the cash office to the safe.

Safe? The door was a good six feet tall and at least three feet wide. It was the type of thing you found in a Quentin Tarantino movie. Garret entered some numbers on a keypad near the face of the vault and slid his thumb over a screen. The door clicked, and he dragged it open.

When Shay pushed the cart toward the open vault, Garret shook his head. "Sorry. Only staff allowed past this door."

Shay stepped back, waiting until Garret walked out and closed the twelve-inch thick door, leaving the trunks and cart inside. He pulled on the handle, and the door locked, the lights on the keypad going red.

Adam's phone dinged. He pulled it out, and a huge grin spread over his face. He didn't even bother looking up from whatever was on the screen. And given the way his eyes slid up and down the small device, shay probably didn't want to know what he was ogling. Or who. "Are we done here?" Adam asked.

"I have to get the forms for you to sign and go over the information," Garret said.

Adam's huge grin deflated. Hell, his whole body practically deflated.

"Shay could sign for everything if you have to be somewhere." Garret actually looked like he'd hope Adam would say yes. And deep down, Shay was okay with that. Spending a few more minutes alone with Garret wasn't exactly a hardship.

"I was going to stay here and see how it's all done, anyway." Shay would take this bullet and let Adam get to whatever was on that text—or more likely sext.

"You sure?" Adam's phone dinged again, and his eyes widened. The grin was gone.

"I wouldn't have offered."

"You're right. Go ahead." He texted something into his phone. The newlyweds were all romance and horndog in Illinois. She could only imagine the texts here in Vegas. No. She didn't want to imagine them.

"Can I go?" Adam asked, eyes on the screen.

"Yes." *Please, and take your creepy smile and bulging...eyeballs with you.*

"Thanks." Adam turned to Garret. "We'll see you tomorrow night at the bachelor party."

"Yeah, man. See you."

Adam ran—literally ran—out the door. Shay swore she could see the escape swirls in the air like on the cartoons. "So, what do I need to do?"

Garret pulled off his suit coat, hanging it on the

back of a chair. He unbuttoned his sleeves and rolled them above his forearms. Good gracious. Muscles danced and bunched as he pulled out a chair and motioned to her. "Have a seat while I get this together. I'll just need a signature."

She sat in the chair across from him and watched as he grabbed a form and wrote, grabbed and wrote. The only sound was the pen scraping against the page. Well, that and the sound of her heart beating against her ribs. She couldn't help it.

He looked edible—when he wasn't talking. His arms inched back and forth as he wrote, the muscles bunching and bulging. The man was every women's wet dream, complete with happy ending.

Her heart thumped. He could probably hear every renegade beat telling him she wanted him. Not that she did. Oh, who was she kidding—she so did. But she didn't need him to *know* she did.

"If you can sign and date this, you are all set." He handed over the paperwork as the door whipped open.

"Why are you still here?" A man in the requisite black suit and tie barreled through the door. He wasn't bad looking, with black hair, olive skin, and muscles in all the right places. They must have a great gym onsite.

New guy looked at Shay and smiled. Geez. He had one of those white smiles—all bright and dazzling. The dental plan at this place must be fantastic, too.

"Just finishing up the jewelry paperwork."

"So, are you one of the cops with the jewelry company?" The new guy hadn't taken his eyes off her. And not in a creepy, stalker kind of way. No. He drank her in like a fine wine. Interesting. "Is it true you flew all the way from Chicago to loan these rich jerkoffs millions of dollars in jewelry?"

"Rick..." Garret's tone was all business.

"It's okay." Shay was having a problem with the concept herself. Who loaned out that much jewelry to flaky stars? Couldn't they afford to buy their own jewelry? "Yes, it's all true. Cop. Chicago. Jerkoffs. Jewelry. All of it."

"Wow. Good luck with that. I don't know if they'll be able to find their jewelry in the morning. I just saw Georgiana Drake throwing up outside the club. And the jewelry...? Let's just say you'll need some diamond cleaner, although most of it landed on a palm tree by the pool. Does puke nourish trees or kill them?"

Ick. "Probably kill them. Maybe if you pick up some of it up in a jar, you can sell it online."

"Hey, that's not a bad idea." He seemed genuinely interested in the idea.

Shay looked down and widened her eyes to stop them from rolling in her head. Yes, she threw it out there, but it was a joke. A bad joke, and an even worse idea, a horrible idea. And gross.

Garret didn't even bother stopping his eyes from rolling. "Don't you have work to do?"

"Yeah, boss." Rick turned to Shay. "How long are you in town?"

Garret pointed out the door. "Rick. Work. Now."

Rick pulled out a card and handed it to Shay. "Give me a call if you're looking for something to do tomorrow night. I know this great Thai place."

She smiled as he walked away. Not the brightest bulb, but he was nice to look at. And he gave her his number. Overall, a win.

"You can throw that out." Garret held up a small garbage can.

"Throw what out?"

He set the plastic receptacle in front of her. "His card. It's not like you're going to use it."

She looked at the flashy black laminated card with Security Consultants at the top, and Rick Drakos along the bottom. From what Sal had said during one of their downtimes, the hotel didn't actually employ the security team, a consultant company did. "Why wouldn't I?"

"Really, you're going to call him?"

"Why not? He was nice, good-looking…"

"And he'll sleep with anything that moves." He tapped the papers in front of her and handed her a pen. "You don't want any part of that."

She leaned over and signed her name. How did he know what she wanted part of? It wasn't his choice. She made her own decisions—and the fact that she probably didn't want anything to do with Rick and his indiscriminate sleeping choices were not Garret's business.

The heat of his body seeped into her back. When had he come up behind her? His breath whispered across her cheek. "Trust me."

The deep timbre of his voice and his hot breath sliding along her neck shivered straight down her spine and curled her toes. He was so close. So good.

She entered the date on the form. Maybe. She at least entered numbers. Maybe. She couldn't seem to think straight. Her mind couldn't get off the words, *trust me*. She really didn't want to trust him. She shouldn't trust him. Right? "Why should I trust you?"

He stepped back and picked up the signed forms. "Why shouldn't you trust me?" His scowl was right there. Right in her face. She was having a hard time focusing on his words when his lips looked so good. So pink, plump, and completely edible. If he would just stop talking...

"Why wouldn't you trust me?" His tone softened, and that scowl was replaced with a smirk.

Jackass.

"Trust is two ways," Shay said. "You haven't shown me any trust. You didn't trust me with the jewelry heist information. What else haven't you told me?" She slid Rick's card in her pocket. Not that she'd use it, but Garret didn't need to know that.

He ran a hand over the back of his neck. "Nothing. I haven't left out anything. If I thought those burglaries had anything to do with you or the jewelry, I would have mentioned it. The perp took advantage of vulnerabilities in the casino's vault procedures. Somehow, they've known when the vault is open and when the security staff is busy."

"So, you think it's an inside job."

"Maybe." His eyebrows furrowed as frustration overtook his features. He didn't seem to like unanswered questions. Join the club. They pissed her off too.

"Is the security consultant company for those hotels the same?"

"No. They have different companies, but security in Vegas is a small world. Everyone knows each other. Most of the security staff has worked at more than one of the hotels or casinos." He sighed. "But between Sal, Mary, and I, we've locked everything down, just in case the perp worked here at some time. We've rearranged the schedule. We're on top of it. That's why I didn't bother your team with the information. I wasn't keeping it from you."

He looked so sincere with his slumped shoulders. And adorable. Did she mention how adorable he looked? His rolled-up sleeves and open collar showed enough skin to make it interesting—namely a crumb of blond chest hair against his sun-tanned neck. When had he lost the tie? It was a good look on him.

She just couldn't stay mad. Not when what he'd said made sense. "Okay."

"Okay?"

"Okay. I trust you." And she did. She had no idea why, but there was something about him. And it wasn't just the green eyes, although they were pretty. It was the knowledge they seemed to hold in their depths. It was the way those eyes seemed to look deep inside her.

"Good." He smiled and slipped the signed forms into a file folder on top of the desk. "Are you heading back to your room?"

"Yes." She sighed. Back to the suite she was sharing with three other women—three women who would probably be up all night talking again. With her luck, they'd start painting each other's toenails, or pillow fighting. Is that what women did these days during a sleepover? With the exception of last night, she hadn't actually been on one since high school—although it had been a quiet night. But that was mostly because they were exhausted after their flight.

Maybe they'd be exhausted again. Shay knew she was. The suite had four bedrooms, so if Shay wanted, she could hide in her room. If the giggling women would even let her.

Garret rolled down his sleeves and slipped on his jacket, tucking his tie into the pocket. He opened the door and held it for Shay. She followed him down the back halls, up the stairs and through heavy double doors into the flashing lights of the casino floor. The stench of booze hit her nostrils as they crossed the crowded floor and headed over to the main set of elevators.

"Hey, baby, need a date?" A blonde with more makeup than Bozo the Clown slid her hand along Garret's arm. She looked over to Shay standing next to him and winked. Winked? Really. What was she looking for, a threesome?

Garret reached into his front pocket and smiled. "I'm covered. What's your name?"

"Debbie."

"Debbie." He showed his security badge to Debbie, who was no longer doing Dallas but apparently had moved to Vegas. "I suggest you find another casino to, uh, hawk your wares."

"Your loss, sugar." She swiveled on narrow hips.

"And, Debbie? Don't come back here." He slid his badge back in his pocket. "Next time, I'll call Metro."

"Why would you call the cops?" She leaned her head over her shoulder and batted her eyelashes. Why did every woman feel an urge to do that in Garret's presence? "I'm just looking for a good time."

"Look elsewhere. Not in my hotel." He watched her walk out the front door of the casino before turning to Shay. "Sorry about that."

"Does that happen a lot?"

"Which? Me getting propositioned, or me kicking out the local escorts?"

"Both."

"Not as much as you'd think. Most of the women know to avoid the cops and any kind of security. But if I'm just hanging out on the Strip I get quite a few offers."

"Sounds interesting."

"Not really. You know how it is. I'm sure you have professional escorts back in Chicago. It's sad. I feel for anyone who thinks that's the only thing they have to offer the world." Garret laid a hand on the small of her back. Warm tingles spread out from where his fingers touched.

He didn't turn toward the front doors. He didn't head to the parking garage. He kept going toward the elevators. Maybe he lived here. Did employees actually live at the hotels, or was that just something on television? "Are you staying at the hotel?"

"I have a condo over in the residence tower." His hand dropped, leaving a cold handprint on her back.

He pointed toward a building on the other side of the pool outside. That explained why he hadn't headed for the exit, but it didn't explain why he was standing there with her. Maybe it was chivalry, walking her to the elevator. But she didn't want him to feel obligated to walk her any farther. It had been a long day followed by a longer night. And she was a Chicago police officer, for goodness sake. She could handle herself.

"Well...um...thanks for walking me to the elevators. I can find my way back to the room."

"I don't mind." He hit the button for the twentieth floor. Her floor. She'd never told him her floor.

"How do you know what floor I'm on?"

The elevator door popped open and Garret held it open as she walked in. His eyes searched the floor for something, probably his answer. She'd caught her share of people caught in the act. What he was caught in the act of doing, she had no idea. But at least he had the common courtesy to look embarrassed. "I have access to all the hotel guest information."

Yeah, that didn't answer her question. "So you've memorized all the guests' room numbers. Aren't there like over three thousand rooms? Who's in room 2125?"

His eyes dropped lower before moving up to hers. "I haven't memorized them all. I checked yours. I wanted to make sure they gave you a good room."

They stood together in the elevator. The smell of that spiced eucalyptus wrapped around her. He smelled so damn good. It should be illegal.

He turned to her and smiled. Smiled. It was definitely illegal to call what he did just a smile. Gorgeous white teeth between beautiful pink lips. Ugh. She spun away and stared at a poster on the doors. The buffet was open till ten. Good to know.

The elevator buzzed upward, and with a ding, the doors flew open on a dark hallway.

Garret's hand found its way to the crook of her back again. The sizzle of his touch, just his touch was enough to make her insides burn. If just his hand did that to her body, what would the rest of his body do to her?

Nothing. His body would do nothing to her. She swore her lady parts wept at the self-imposed embargo.

"I'm really not a stalker or anything. I wanted to make sure you *all* were staying at the hotel. All the cops from Chicago. It makes it easier to get ahold of you if there's a problem."

They walked down the hall, and the elevator gave a soft ding as the doors closed. His fingers moved back and forth, up and down the center of her back. So gentle. The warmth seeped through her shirt, her heart beating double-time. Geez. She was like some horny teenager, getting excited about some guy touching her. It didn't matter he had large, warm hands that sent waves jolting through her body. It didn't matter she hadn't felt this way in a very long time. None of that mattered.

And none of that made it okay that her core was pulsing beneath his touch. It wasn't okay. Not at all. He wasn't someone she could get serious about—if she was looking to get serious. Not that she was. But she wasn't a hit it and quit it kind of girl, either.

Shay walked along the bright blue carpeting. Silver sconces lit the walls.

It was quiet. No one was milling about the halls. No sounds. It was like Shay and Garret were the only ones on the planet. Which was dangerous. With the pink lips, white teeth, and warm hands, it was taking every ounce of control to keep her hands to herself. This was not like her. She was a cop. A detective. She didn't need to control her actions. She was above that. She knew better.

But Garret did things to her... Made her forget her rules. Made her forget she wasn't looking for a man, a relationship, or a one-night stand. The minute his hands slid along her skin, she became putty.

What the hell was wrong with her?

GARETT DIDN'T WANT to let her go. He wanted to wrap her in his arms, feel her, taste her. Although, after his announcement that he accommodation-stalked her, putting his hands anywhere other than her back would probably lead to a jab to the throat. He'd rather not have the wind knocked out of him this late at night. Or ever, really. But after the day he'd had, he didn't have the wherewithal to defend himself.

In fact, he was probably taking his life in his hands touching her back. Guiding her. But dammit she felt so good, so sweet, he couldn't stay away.

Shay turned, and her eyes locked on Garret's. Soft.

Kind. He could seriously get lost in them. They were warm and comforting.

It just showed that everything about her was sweet. Her smile. Her eyes. Her lips.

His body hummed just thinking about those lips. He wanted to take a nibble—just a small one. He wanted to explore those lips. Taste them. Feel them.

Just once. Get it out of his system. Cure his curiosity.

"So." She smiled.

"So."

Her eyes found his before they looked away and focused on the hideous carpet. He knew he should drop his hand, but he couldn't. He didn't want this— whatever this was— to end.

"Thanks for the escort." Her eyes widened, and her cheeks darkened. "I didn't mean *escort* escort... I mean, thank you for the assist. Getting me to my room without incident." Pulling away, she shook her head and angled her hand in her pocket, pulling out a plastic card. "Just, thanks."

She stood there toying with the key card, her long, delicate fingers sliding the card back and forth, back and forth. Everything about her was hotter than the Mirage volcano. And he was inches from erupting.

Her tongue slid out and ran along her bottom lip. She was killing him. The blush on her cheeks. The shine on her lips.

For the love of...

He reached over and pulled her to him. Her chest rose and fell against his. Her eyes searched his and her hands wrapped around his shirt. She didn't push him away. She didn't tell him to stop.

He took that as a go.

His mouth slowly lowered to hers, his lips sweeping gently before pulling back. He wanted to give her time to say no. He wanted to take this slow. With a small smile, she pulled her lip into her mouth—and sucked.

Fuck slow.

He dove in, stroking his mouth over hers. She sighed as her lips parted. *Yeah, we're a go.* He mingled his tongue with hers before sliding his mouth down her neck. Desperate to taste every last inch of her. And she did not disappoint. She was sweet and salty and so hot.

Her body melded with his until every single curve and edge slid along him. Her breasts rubbed up and down along his chest, her hips grinding into his growing interest. And it was growing. And it hurt. It wanted to be deep inside of her.

"There you are." The one they called Julie stuck her head out of the door to the room. At least he thought it was Julie. His eyes were currently stuck on crossed. "We were worried about you."

Shay jumped back and attempted a smile. She wasn't successful. It was hard to pull off the innocent look with wild eyes and a flushed face. Not to mention swollen lips.

Pride warred with the blue balls he was currently fighting. He did that. He brought that wild to her eyes. He brought that plump swelling to her lips.

Damn, the woman was fine.

"I'll be right in." Shay smiled at Julie and then turned to Garret. "I should go in."

"Yeah." No. "I'm sure you need your rest." Like he'd rest. Not that he was complaining. Remembering her lips on his, her body pressed against him—rest was overrated.

"Yeah, it's been a long day." She leaned her hand on the opened door of the room.

"Wait." He reached out and touched her arm. The electricity practically hummed between them. That taste didn't cure his curiosity, only made his desire for her stronger. It made the next words so much easier to say. "Why don't we go to dinner tomorrow night?"

"I don't think that's a good idea."

"Why not? Planning on calling Rick?" He might have said that as a joke, but dammit if that didn't actually twist something inside of him. It was not pleasant. Idiot.

"No." She smiled, actually smiled. It practically lit up the drab hallway. Hell, it seemed to light up his world and make him forget what an idiot he was.

"Then why?" He ran a finger down the side of her face. He would never get tired of touching her.

"We're going to the Profane from Brisbane show tomorrow night for Allison's bachelorette party."

He forgot about that. He'd been invited to the bachelor side of the party by Adam himself.

"Heaven forbid I interfere with disrobing Aussies." He couldn't help but smile. He'd seen his share of disrobing women in this town. Bachelor parties were known for them, and all his friends were happily married.

Someday, he'd like to join their ranks. Again. Since his first marriage hadn't worked out the way he'd hoped. Then again, who hoped to get divorced? Sometimes, though, he wondered if he could go through all of that again. But touching Shay. Looking at Shay. He was starting to think it might be worth it.

This woman had some janky effect on him. She had him questioning all his choices—and apparently begging. "How about a drink after the show?"

"I'm not sure what we're going to do." She propped herself against the partially open door and played with the card in her hand. Did he mention how hot it was as she slid her hand back and forth…? All right, enough of that. He was going to need an Arctic shower as it was without revisiting thoughts of those hands.

"I'm sure I'll see you around, then." He turned on his heel and headed down the hall. He'd made his point. He'd asked her out. She shot him down. He wasn't about to beg. Again.

"Good night, Garret."

He turned around. She hadn't left the doorway. She stood there, watching him go. "Good night."

She opened the door and walked in. The click of the latch was the only sound. She was gone. And she had no interest in him. Maybe some interest, but as soon as her friend showed up she'd pulled away.

So what? What exactly did he expect? For them to become besties, lovers, boyfriend and girlfriend? That wasn't going to happen. He wasn't looking for a relationship or a long-distance friendship. None of that.

Somehow, he had an eerie feeling he'd never be able to let go if they took it to that level. He never thought he'd be saying this, but thank goodness for Julie and her cock-blocking ways.

Too bad his cock didn't share in that excitement.

Honestly, his heart wasn't all that thrilled either. Which was exactly why he knew that stopping whatever happened with Shay was the right answer. No matter how much it hurt.

CHAPTER EIGHT

SATURDAY AFTERNOON, and Shay stared at herself in the bathroom mirror through a fog of hairspray. They each had their own bathroom, but somehow everyone had congregated in Shay's. Getting ready separately wasn't as much as fun as doing it together. Who knew? Not her. She would have been fine primping without all the smog.

Although it was nice to have them around. She was kind of getting into the gossip. But she'd never admit it. She would deny that factoid with her dying breath.

Shay grabbed her jojoba oil from the bag on the counter, bumping Julie—who had a curling iron stuck in her hair while she doused herself in hairspray. This felt dangerous. Like all they needed was someone to light a match and the building would explode *Die Hard*-style.

Julie removed the curling iron and picked up a comb. *Uncle.* Shay left the asphyxiation chamber and parked herself in front of the mirror on the far wall of the suite. As far away from the cloud as she could get without leaving her bedroom.

She opened the oil, squeezing some into her palms and sliding her fingers through her shoulder-length hair. The ebony strands perked to life with every swipe. She wasn't exactly a girly-girl, but this was one thing she couldn't live without. Without the oil, her hair was dull and dry.

"Holy crap, is it loud in there." Brook ducked out of the billowing spray tumbling from the bathroom. And it was. The women were talking about everything from how many drinks they planned on consuming to how many dollar bills they wanted to stuff down the gorgeous Aussies' pants. Between that and Allison's phone, that chirped neverending, silence was in short supply.

"Did she get the caterer all sorted out?" Shay asked, following Brook out of the bathroom. That was the last call. Allison's wedding back in Chicago this upcoming weekend was falling apart. And Allison was here in Vegas, stressing out.

"Yeah, they're going to substitute chicken for the pork loin on some of the plates. What a mess." Brook dropped onto the bed and fell backward. "I'm so tired."

Agreed. Shay could relate. She was already in need of a nap. This morning the celebrities, or their assistants, had returned the jewelry, and all of the bling was nestled back in the safe. All sixty-seven pieces—which shocked the hell out of Shay. How many years could a person live in one of the un-extradite-able countries with the money from one of those baubles? Luckily, no one had decided to test that out.

The jewelry return turned out to be much less involved than the pickup. Most of the celebrities sent their assistants down to do the return, and all the jewelry was in one piece, no stones missing. Overall, it went smooth as Cool Whip. No issues and not too many Garret sightings. And when she had seen him, he was busy.

Which was good. She didn't need the drama. What happened between them last night was amazing, hot, wonderful—a mistake.

"So... What's up with you and Garret?"

Had Shay said all of that out loud? How else would Brook have known about Garret? She hadn't told anyone after she'd gotten to the room, and Julie had gone straight to bed. It's not like they'd had all kinds of time to stand around gossiping today with the jewelry return.

Even if Shay had said all of that out loud, it wasn't going to stop her from playing stupid. "What?" And for the record, she was just playing stupid. No matter how dumb it had been to flirt with Garret, kiss him, and fantasize about his hands all over her body...

Yep, just playing.

"Don't be mad at Joe. He's just worried about you. Wanted me to make sure you know what you're doing."

Perretti? Oh yeah, he might have gotten a glimpse of the flirting portion of the evening. Thankfully, he hadn't seen anything else. "What exactly am I doing?"

"He said, and I quote, you've been eye-humping

Garret since we got here." Brook added air quotes around eye-humping.

"Is eye-humping bad?" Real humping sounded so much better.

"I don't think so, but he seems to think we should be worried."

"And what do you think?"

Brook slid to her side and rested on her elbow, careful to avoid smushing her curls. "I think he's being overprotective. But he gets that way with you. You're his partner. He worries."

"I would think he'd have better things to worry about other than me. Like Stark's upcoming court date."

"Oh God, don't mention that." Brook cringed and flopped back. So much for the curls she'd baked into her hair with a curling iron. But Shay could under-stand. Dennis Maxwell Stark was currently awaiting trial for kidnapping Brook a few months back. Needless to say, Joe had freaked when she was taken and when they'd found her.

"He still has a conniption fit if I want to go out at night by myself," Brook added. "He's getting better, but damn, the boy sure does like to helicopter."

Helicopter. Good word for it. It also was not surprising. Shay had seen Brook after the kidnapping. The bruises, the blood—it had been heartbreaking. She could almost understand Perretti's concern. It hadn't been easy for Shay finding her friend like that, and Perretti was head over heels loopy for the woman. He took it all pretty hard.

"Yes, well I don't want to be on the receiving end of his hovering." Shay ran her hands down the sides of her hair, making sure it stayed in place.

"No one does." Brook lifted her shoulders— at least that was what it looked like while she was flat on the bed. Either that or she was having some kind of fit. "But I'm done being the center of his meltdowns. It's your turn."

"Fantastic." Shay grabbed her money clip and shoved it into her pocket. Her room key and license went into her bra. No purse tonight. Nothing that might get forgotten or lifted as they walked the Strip.

Julie and Allison walked out of the bathroom, their hair teased and makeup heavy. The black spandex and brightly colored leg warmers almost made them look like twins. However, the vest Allison wore over a popped collar shirt was different than the oversized sweater that hung to Julie's knees.

Had Shay forgotten to mention the bachelorette party was themed? Eighties-themed. Not that Shay would complain—although she wanted to. It was Allison's party. Allison's choice. And Shay could admit she looked pretty damn cute right now. Tight blue jeans, white tank top, and a black leather jacket. She was channeling Toni Braxton, circa 1993. So not exactly the eighties. Sue her. It wasn't like anyone cared all that much. And she looked good.

"These are for tonight." Allison went into the closet, clicked a few buttons, and opened the room safe. She took out three black leather boxes, peeked inside the top two, and handed one to her sister. "Brook, this is for you." She offered the second box to Shay. "Shay, this one's for you." The third one went to Julie.

Shay opened the box. A bracelet lined with diamonds sparkled in the center, with a matching necklace surrounding it. It was beautiful. And shiny.

"Wow. Look at me." Julie had already put hers on, a teardrop necklace that fell right between the girls. "It's amazing." And expensive.

Allison smiled and turned to Shay. "Aren't you going to wear yours?"

"Out in public?" Shay never could understand how someone could spend so much money on jewelry—something worn around the neck or wrist—and then wear it where others could steal it. Seemed like an invitation for trouble.

"Yes. We have quite the night planned, and you need to be pampered." Allison walked over to where Shay stood and drew out the necklace. "Here." She wrapped the string of bling around Shay's neck, and the gold tickled her skin as Allison fought with the clasp. "There. You're all set."

The necklace fell just above the top of the tank and sparkled. Just sparkled. No matter which way Shay turned. No matter how she moved, the diamonds caught the light and threw it back in rainbows. "Wow."

"Beautiful." Allison wrapped her arm around Shay. "I wanted to give you all something for helping and for being my bridal party. I'm so glad you all agreed."

Julie played with the bracelet on her wrist. "Of course."

Shay's eyes darted between the necklace and Allison. The jewelry was a loan, right? She wasn't giving these to them. She spun the bracelet and tried to snap the clasp. "This is a loan, right?"

"No. I made these for you." Allison grabbed the two ends of the bracelet and secured it to Shay's wrist. "They're a gift for my friends."

What do you say to that? Shay didn't have a lot of friends. Definitely not girlfriends. Who had time for that? She had the job, a teenage brother, and a grandmother to take care of. She didn't have time to go out. She didn't have people. She had coworkers, mostly male. Although that was changing. There was a time she was the only female detective. They were slowly filling open detective slots with female cops.

Which meant she wasn't the only female at the bar after work. But that didn't mean they were all besties. And the last time Shay had been to the bar after work... Her brother had been in grade school.

"I know it's a little much, but I hope you'll accept it." Allison looked nervous, almost like she was afraid Shay would run away and tell them she didn't want to play with them.

Shay couldn't say no. Allison and Adam were her friends. And she didn't have very many of those these days. She wasn't quite sure when it happened, but it did. Brook was family, and Allison was her sister. So naturally, they were all family to Shay. "Sure."

Allison threw her arms around Shay again. This time, Julie and Brook joined in. It was like the beginning of *The Hangover* where they all stood around and took their first drink to the evening—but here, instead of drinking there were hugs. And hopefully no one would end up roofied by the end of the night.

GARRET SAT in the dark back room of the bar. Soft lighting came from candles in the center of the tables, and track lighting blasted colored streaks across the ceiling. Scantily clad women danced in cages to the deep bass of the dance music thumping the floor.

Club Marimba would have been a great spot for the party, but there was no way Garret was partying where he worked. So they'd trekked down the Strip to another club. The craziness of the country awards was over. Most of the celebrities had headed home with their memories, but that didn't stop the locals and the tourists from looking for a night of debauchery. Everyone liked to test the What Happens in Vegas theory. Thankfully, he was hanging out with the cops from Chicago. They weren't exactly the debauchery type.

"Why aren't we at the strip club? This sucks." Lopez took his drink from the waitress. She wasn't hanging on his every word, which apparently was making Lopez bitchy. Her lack of interest probably had something to do with the rock on her left hand.

"We're not going to a strip club." Byrnes seemed to be getting sick of that question, given the scowl he threw. "The booze is just as fine here."

"Yeah, but there is way too much clothing going on here for a bachelor party."

"No one's stopping you, take it off." Ben Mooring tipped his beer bottle toward Lopez.

"No," Byrnes and Perretti said at the same time as Lopez started unbuttoning his shirt.

"Hey, I'm an equal opportunity nudist," Lopez snarked. "It's not fair to ask them to stop, drop, and pole dance if I'm not willing to do it too."

Garret couldn't help but laugh as Lopez buttoned up his shirt and drank down his beer. This crew was fun. He was actually having a good time. Hell, how long had it been since he'd had a good time? He couldn't even remember. He raised his tumbler of Jim Beam and took a sip. The club was known for their selection of bourbon, so he always partook when he stopped by. The sweet from the sugar offset the burn from the bourbon. Perfect mix.

Lopez popped up from his chair. "I'm going to get another round. Anyone in?" Everybody either nodded or said yes, and then he was off toward the bar. He made it about twenty feet before getting sidelined by a brunette in a tight sheath dress.

"So, you and Shay, huh?" Perretti asked. He was going for nonchalant, but his tone almost held a big-brother edge. Not that Garret could judge. Sal and Mary were the siblings he never had. He could see himself pulling out that tone if anyone ever tried to start something with Mary.

Garret just gave a quick nod as he raised his drink. What was there to say? He had no idea what he and Shay were. Not enough to defend it to big brother. Not enough to label it. Hell, it was a kiss. A great kiss, and he couldn't wait to do it again, but that's all it was.

"What's going on there?" Byrnes joined in on the inquisition.

Garret swirled the drink in his hand. He didn't think sharing his "only a kiss" theory with the Brothers Grim would win him points. "Why don't you ask her?"

"Yeah, right." Perretti laughed, actually laughed. "You obviously don't know her very well. She'd kick my ass."

"Yeah, she would." Byrnes leaned over and punched Perretti in the shoulder. "Between Brook and her, Joe here doesn't need to ever need to make a decision. They tell him what to do."

"Pot. Kettle." Perretti leaned back against his chair. "Don't get your leash caught on any of the waitresses. Allison wouldn't like that."

"Allison can put a leash on me any day of the week." Byrne's smile actually glowed. He was so whipped. Or, apparently, shackled.

Ben Mooring snorted as he took in a drink. "You actually make that leash look pretty good."

Adam smiled. "Speaking of leashes, any luck with Julie? I saw you two talking yesterday."

"I wouldn't say what we were doing was talking, more like playing telephone through Shay. She wouldn't even speak to me. She would only talk to Shay." Mooring made a face before taking a deep swig of beer. "It was like being back in grade school passing notes."

"She'll come around." Byrnes slapped him on the back. "Allison forgave you."

"Yeah, but how long did that take? Julie's a tougher sell."

Garret had seen the way Julie glared at the guy. Whatever he did put him at the top of her shit-list and she didn't seem to be changing her position any time soon. The guy had an uphill battle, and he looked destroyed by it.

There was a part of Garret that didn't want to do the whole relationship thing again. He knew that battle. He'd waged it. He'd lost. After all the dust had settled and the death toll counted, he'd been hollow, destroyed and alone.

But then he'd look at his friends or his parents. They made it work. They were happy. Happiness was out there. He just needed to find it.

Lopez somehow made it back in record time, laden with beer bottles and a round of shots. "Dartboard's open, but we have to go now. Anyone in?"

Garret nodded before tossing back the shot—Jim Beam Kentucky Fire—and the guys downed theirs before following Lopez to the back of the room where a dartboard hung. A redheaded waitress with a small waist and big chest stood in front. Her uniform skirt rode high on her thighs.

"Thanks for guarding our board, sweetheart." Lopez set the tray of beers on the high-top table across from the board and wrapped an arm around the busty barmaid. "Can we get some of those nachos you were talking about earlier?"

"Sure thing." She shimmied away.

Lopez picked up three red darts. "Since no one's getting naked, let's play."

Garret was exhausted. He'd been on the go since five this morning while the jewelry was returned and the celebs checked out. This was a standard weekend at the hotel, but that still left him worn out. Not that he had time to sleep. Stacks of paperwork waited for him back at the office.

Mooring finished his beer and put the empty on the table. "Look guys, I'm going to head back to the room."

"I'll head back with you," Garret said. "I need to get back to my office anyway."

"Hell no, the party's just started." Lopez pushed one of the new beers toward Mooring. "I got you another drink."

"Stick around." Byrnes looped his arm around Garret's shoulders. "A few more drinks, then we'll probably just go pick up the women."

Probably. Garret eyed the drink Lopez held out. A couple of hours. He could manage a few hours. After all, he hadn't been out just for fun in months. What could possibly go wrong in a few hours?

THE LIGHTS PULSED as the male dancer strutted out from behind the curtain, carrying a metal chair. Heavy metal music blared as his muscles rippled. Shay could see every single muscle actually ripple since all he wore was a thin Speedo. There was nothing left for the imagination. He was basically letting it all hang out.

Not that she was complaining. What hung out looked pretty damn fine. He had a six-pack—no, make it eight—arrowing down into a V pointing to an impressive bulge. The tattoos lining his arms winked at her.

He spun the chair into place at the center of the stage and strutted around behind it. Raising his hand to his forehead to shade his eyes, he scanned the audience. He smirked, and his other hand pointed right at Allison, his fingers giving her a come-hither wave. Allison looked around, but his eyes didn't leave her, and his hand stopped moving just long enough to point at her.

"Happy bachelorette party!" Brook grabbed Allison's hand and dragged her out of her chair before pushing her to the stairs at the side of the stage.

"You did this." Allison tried to hold on to Brook as muscle guy pulled her slowly up the stairs.

Brook shook her off and sat down in the comfort of her chair. "You're welcome."

Allison's face was bright red. What could be seen of it, anyway. Her neck was scrunched, and she apparently was trying to hide in her shirt, which wasn't quite working. Muscles sat her down on the metal chair before sitting himself down on her lap—facing her. His body rubbed against hers as she laughed. She wrapped her arm around him and slapped his ass. Then giggled before she slapped a hand over her eyes.

The women in the audience hooted and hollered as the male dancer sat on her lap and rotated his hips. His goodies bumped back and forth against Allison before he stood up. His manhood poked her in the face as he gyrated up and down—up and down. If she wasn't care-ful, she'd have a large mushroom bruise on her fore-head. Have fun explaining that one to Adam.

Now Shay could admit she'd love a closer look at the male-hotness on the stage, but not that close, and not on a stage in front of all these screaming women.

Muscles spun away from the chair, shaking his Speedo like a maraca as he circled Allison—who had both hands clapped over her face. Probably to avoid putting an eye out with his manhood. He peeled one hand free and helped her stand, bringing her fingertips to his lips and leading her over to the stairs. Before he let her go, he dipped her back, her hair trailing over his arm and almost covering the cute little teddy bear tattoo on his forearm. With a caress of her cheek, he left her at their table and moved on to the next unsuspecting bachelorette.

"Oh my goodness! I cannot believe you did that." Allison laughed and threw a napkin at her sister. She was an absurd shade of red from ear to ear. Heck, even her arms appeared to be glowing. If Santa knew about her Glo Worm superpower, he'd have never even bothered with Rudolph.

"Believe it, because there is so much more." Brook held out four bright orange shots that she'd just gotten from a gorgeous waiter. "Sex on the beach. And him."

"Hey, baby." Gorgeous waiter looked at Allison. "I'm Rusty." He sat in the chair next to Julie and Shay. The look of horror on Allison's face was hilarious—mostly because the nightmare wasn't happening to Shay.

Reminder: Never, ever let Brook plan a bachelorette party. Not enough.

Reminder revisited: Never, ever tell Brook about any impending marriages or holidays or birthdays.

Not that Shay had any plans to get married, but if she did, the chance was too great she'd end up in a place like this with Muscles' manhood in her face. Nope.

"Good evening ladies. I'm Drae." Another love god sat down next to Allison. He was black as night and hot as flame. He had gorgeous teeth. White and straight. And the muscles—dreamy. No other words would do... if Shay could even think of any other words.

"So, you're the bride." Dreamy—Drae, his name was Drae—leaned into Allison and smiled. Smiled. Holy smokes. With his great teeth, rounded cheeks and large...well, everything—he looked like Luke Cage with dreads. His large hand rested on Allison's shoulder.

And my, what large hands you do have. Too bad he was sitting. Shay was curious if the handles matched the knob.

"So, ladies, how do you know the bride?"

Muscles cousin—what was his name again? Oh, yeah, Rusty—Rusty leaned into Julie and Shay. He had a nice smile, but his teeth weren't as nice. Too many gaps. Nothing like Garret.

Wait. What?

Not like Garret. Nothing like *Dreamy* over there. Dreamy had the nice teeth. He smiled again, his front tooth slightly tilted to the side. Not that it mattered. That was so superficial. What mattered was on the inside.

Having the same goals, hopes, and dreams. That's what mattered. Not the angle of his incisors. And looking at the dark glistening man across the table— yeah, they'd have a lot in common.

"I love a woman who knows how to be a woman," Dreamy said in a deep baritone. "All women should be showered with diamonds."

Or maybe not. Diamonds were not this girl's best friend. In fact, with the exception of tonight, Shay rarely even wore jewelry. Not that that mattered. She was sure Dreamy and her would hit it off.

"And look at you rocking those fuck-me pumps. I'm

a sucker for coming home from a long night at work to a woman in heels, satisfying my every need."

Um...

Should she be wearing heels, or should she be barefoot and pregnant? Maybe he'd like her making his dinner and cleaning his house while she sucked him off. Okay, maybe they weren't exactly compatible. Or maybe she was overreacting. Maybe this was all an act, just what he said to women to get them all hot and bothered.

But even so, if anyone wanted to rev her engine, mentioning how she should be standing ready to satisfy his needs was the total wrong way to go. *He* should be on the ready with a bath, a massage, and a giant O waiting for her after a long day on the Chicago streets.

Shay stared as Rusty flirted with Julie and Drae hung on Allison and Brook. Thankfully, Shay's chair was far enough away that no one bothered her and she could just watch. She loved to watch... Wait, that sounded really bad.

She loved to watch *people*. People watch. She liked to watch them interact, watch their actions. She loved to try to figure out what made them tick. Sometimes she looked at the bad guys and knew what they were going through, or at least she could see why they'd done what they did.

But not always. And that *not always* was what intrigued her.

"I'm exhausted." Julie's announcement pulled Shay out of her head and back to the club. "I'm going back to the room."

"It's too early." Brook tilted back another shot. Dreamy seemed to have disappeared, and Rusty was standing with his arm around Julie. She wasn't going back to the room with him. Was she?

"Not for me." Julie smiled up at Rusty.

"I have to get back to work, but I'd really like to see you. Can I give you my number?" Rusty smiled.

Julie handed him her phone and he typed into the screen. A ringback tone came through as he probably called his own cell phone.

He handed it back. "I'll call you tomorrow."

"I look forward to it." Julie clasped the phone to her chest, a faraway look on her face—starry eyes, goofy grin. She was loving this, obviously, loving the attention and the admiration. After the headache that had been her relationship with Ben, Shay wasn't surprised. Ben was a great guy and he'd helped out immensely with the jewelry, but he didn't have a great track record with women. Namely, he treated Julie like crap. The girl needed a win, and muscled gods were always a win.

"Ladies, it's been fun." Rusty walked away from the table and slipped into the back while Julie grabbed her purse.

"You can't leave until you tell us all about tall and sexy. Exchanging numbers?" Brook leaned in.

"Tomorrow."

Brook's skeptical eyebrow raise must have compelled Julie to say, "I promise. I have to call the house and see how Cody's doing, and then I'm going to relax in the quiet a bit. I don't get that very often." As a single mother, Julie didn't get a lot of downtime.

Speaking of, Shay could use some phone time with her brother. Check on him—while she still could.

Shay's ex-husband got along with Shawn, so he was keeping an eye on things, but that didn't mean she wanted to sit back and wait. Taking a few minutes to call home sounded like a good idea.

"I'll head back with you." Shay stood up. "No one should be wandering the streets alone." Especially with the bling hanging around their necks.

"We should be right behind you. The guys are coming here after the show." Brook leaned back as the lights lowered for the next dance.

Shay and Julie squeezed past the tables of screaming women into the desert night air. It was so much cooler outside without all the panting. "Taxi or walk?"

Julie looked up into the sky and smiled. "Walk."

"Good choice." Shay turned down Las Vegas boulevard toward their hotel. Tonight had been fun, but Shay was tired. She wanted to sleep or maybe see Garret before she slid into bed—or even better, slide into bed with Garret.

She sighed. She'd given up on pretending to be surprised when her mind went there with all the naughty things she'd like to do to Garret. Her body wanted to go there. Her mind was going there. Why fight it?

She'd been surrounded by nice-looking men in thongs, and her mind went back to Garret. How was that possible? He'd burrowed in, and he didn't seem to be leaving her anytime soon. Maybe it was time to throw caution to the wind and bury its body in the desert.

It was time to start enjoying her vacation in the city of sin. And she knew just who she wanted to share that sin with.

PEOPLE YELLED as the New York Yankees scored another run. Shit. He'd put the money from his last heist on the game and the Yankees were going to fuck it all up. As the bar crowd high-fived, the phone in his pocket vibrated. He had to take this. He'd been blowing his brother off for weeks. But who could blame him? His brother was a dick. He slid out of the booth and made his way through the crowd, outside to the desert air. "Hey."

"'Hey'? That's all you can say to me?"

"It's a common greeting. What do you want?" The neon of the strip pulsed as people bobbed up and down Las Vegas Boulevard.

"I know not to expect anything from you, Scott." His brother sighed. "But we're giving Mom a trip to Hawaii next month to spread Dad's ashes."

"How brownnosing of you." If his brother didn't stop soon, his nose would be permanently tinted. Then his perfect wife and perfect kids would leave, messing up his perfect job and perfect life.

The thought made him smile.

"It's not brownnosing. Mom is having a hard time."

A hard time? What kind of hard time? "Is Mom

okay?" He didn't like to hear his mom wasn't doing well. His dad might have been a useless waste of space, but his mom had always been there for him.

"No. She's not. Which you'd know if you got your head out of your ass long enough to come and visit. Dad's death has been hard on her."

"So you buy her happiness with a trip alone?" That was always his brother's way. Buy things off. Send them away. Being sent away sucked.

His brother sighed. "No. We need to get her out of the house for a while. We're all going to Hawaii. It's a family trip. She wants you to come too."

A trip to Hawaii with the family sounded like torture. "I can't."

"If it's about the money, I'll pay. I just want Mom to be happy."

"I don't want your money, brother." Although he had no idea how he would pay for a trip to Hawaii, knowing his brother's expensive taste. There was no way they'd be at some bargain hotel. He'd pick the largest, most expensive place on the island.

"Fine. I'll loan it to you. But come with. We need this time to heal. Mom needs you."

Nothing on this planet could get him to shell out that kind of money, except for his mother. "If she needs me, I'll be there."

"Great. I'll send you the details. And Scott, don't ruin this."

Before he had a chance to say anything the line went dead. Self-righteous son of a bitch. And people wondered why he hated his brother.

But whether he liked the creep or not, he had to do this for his mom. Another cheer from inside the bar. If the Yankees kept playing this well they would never cover the spread.

And he needed that money now. He had a trip to Hawaii to pay for and no money to do it. He needed cash fast, and he needed weeks to case a vault. Okay, maybe he had to aim a little lower. And right now, he was aiming at the necklaces on the women leaving the club across the street. The blonde's hair was up away from her neck, which gave him the perfect view of his next mark.

He'd watch her, follow her to her hotel and wait for her to be alone. He'd take what he needed.

Just like he'd done before.

THE WALK WAS NICE, but being back at the hotel was nicer. Shay and Julie opened the glass doors to the casino. The high-pitched bings and dings were the first thing to punch Shay in the face. The second was Susie Safari hanging on Garret's arm.

Seriously? Susie, or whatever her name really was, was hanging on his arm laughing as she stared into his eyes. And Garret was laughing, too, lapping up her eye-stroking like a dog in heat.

There went that daydream. No sin in Sin City for her. She didn't take sleazy seconds.

Shay guided Julie to the elevators, taking care to avoid Garret and his lapdog, heading for the car that would take them high into the building and far away from all the BS.

"Shit," Julie whispered as Ben walked around the corner.

Shit. Shay agreed. Ben was great. Julie was an amazing woman. But put these two together and you got a toddler and kitten—one was usually trying to bite the other while the other pulled its tail.

Ben's face was almost comical when he saw Julie. He went from sad to happy to sad in the blink of an eye. His lips performed their own version of the wave as the sides curved down and up and down and up and finally landed on down. "Hey, Julie. Can we talk?"

"Ben, there's nothing to talk about." Julie pressed the up button five, maybe ten too many times. Too bad the elevator didn't come quicker depending on pressing urgency. Someone should invent that. Everyone was already doing it anyway.

The door dinged, and Shay followed Julie inside. And—surprise—so did Ben.

"There is." He leaned toward her.

"I think you said everything you needed to say. If you really wanted to talk about this, about us, you could have. How many times? But you left, just walked away." He'd disappeared for over a year, Shay knew.

"I'm sorry. I was a total jackass, but I was upset and hurt."

"Well, now I'm upset. I'm hurt." Tears pooled in Julie's eyes, spilling down her cheek.

Shay hated being here. Standing off to the side like a voyeur watching them fall apart. It was heartbreaking and awful. And suddenly quiet. Neither one talked. Ben looked miserable. But then, so did Julie.

Silence surrounded them as the door dinged again and opened. Shay made her way to the room, trying to leave enough space for Julie and Ben to figure out their shit in private. Julie didn't seem all that keen on space or privacy, and followed closely behind. Close, hah. If Shay stopped fast, she'd have a Julie wedged up her ass.

Shay slid the room card through the reader and the door popped open. She pushed inside and made a beeline for the bathroom. "I'm going to wash my hands." She turned to see Ben leaning against the door-frame. Yep. They needed alone time.

"Don't go." Julie's eyes pleaded. How could Shay walk away when her friend looked so upset?

"Please, Julie. Please talk to me." Ben reached out, but pulled his hand back when Julie glared at it.

Julie stomped over to the closet where her suitcase was stashed and yanked out a pair of pajamas. She stared at her hands as they worried over the fabric. The frown on her face, the pinch in her eyes—she looked so sad. "Ben. I don't know what you want me to say."

A crash followed by a groan came from the door-way. Ben lay on the floor, clutching his head. Someone, Shay swore it was a man—big hands, broad shoulders—stepped over Ben, his face covered in a ski mask. He aimed his glare and a gun at Julie.

"Let's all calm down." Shay held her hands out. "What do you want? No one needs to get hurt here."

The gun in Ski Mask's left hand wobbled and

lowered about an inch as he lunged for Julie. yanking her necklace off.

"Don't!" Julie screamed, her hand flying to her neck as he yanked her necklace off.

Shay couldn't have said it better herself. She moved fast. Crossed the room in two strides, but she couldn't get there fast enough. He swung around to face her, his left hand—the one with the gun—rising. She couldn't let him aim. She couldn't let him shoot.

She was close, but not close enough to grab the gun, so she spin-kicked instead. Her foot connected, and the gun flew. She pivoted toward him and moved in closer, putting her between him and the gun.

Yeah, buddy, try and get it. Shay almost wished he would. She needed to burn off some of this adrenaline, and whooping his ass would blaze right through it.

He pulled a knife from a sheath at his lower back and danced in front of Shay. Arrogant prick.

Back home, Shay never went anywhere without a blade or a gun. She was always armed. Vacation Shay was completely unstrapped. And walking around without her weapons was code for "uh duh". She should have known better.

She just had to keep her focus. She was in a room with an armed bad guy, without a weapon. She'd taken down guys like this before.

As Ski Mask guy waved the knife at Shay and lifted it high, a scream came from her right. Julie—rushing forward. Shay appreciated the thought, but now was not the time. "Get back!" Shay yelled.

Julie's eyes went saucer-sized when she saw the

knife, but she didn't stop. Before she could reach the guy, Ben knocked her to the floor.

Shay took advantage of the distraction and punched the guy's left arm. The arm zipped to the right, but the knife didn't drop. She landed another punch, this one in his face. And another.

She was taking down this guy no matter what. Shay spun, intent on knocking that knife to the ground. Before she could land a kick, he grabbed her leg, throwing her off balance. Shay went down, and something hard hit her in the back of the head. Game over.

CHAPTER TEN

SHAY HEARD NOISES. Voices. She was sure of it. She tried to lift her neck. Pain shot through her temples and swirled around her head. She was on the floor. But why she was on her back, on the floor, she had no idea.

"Keep everyone out," a disembodied voice said. Hands roamed over her wrists, checking her hands.

"Everyone's out, Garret, but Adam's outside."

"Let's figure this shit out first before we start bringing anyone in. Did you see the guy who hit you?" Garret. That must be Garret's voice. It sounded so close.

Shoes pounded as someone shuffled along the carpet. "No. The guy had a ski mask." Julie's voice. That was definitely Julie's voice. Who was wearing a mask?

Hands ghosted along her body, stopping at her neck. Garret's voice was so close. "And you know it was a guy, how?"

"Build. Voice. The way he knocked the crap out of

me." Knocked the crap out of? Shit. Someone knocked the crap out of Ben. The masked guy came into the room. Where was he? "And then Shay tried to stop him, but he knocked her down." Julie continued. "I did see a tattoo on his arm."

"A tattoo? I thought you said he was wearing a hoodie."

"He was, but the sleeve got pushed up when he was fighting with Shay. It was right here on his forearm."

"Did you see what it was?"

Ben—Shay was pretty sure it was Ben—said, "It was a bear thing with a sword."

"Did you get a good look? Can you draw it?" Wow. Garret was bossy. Was it wrong Shay found that hot?

"Sure, I can try."

"Okay, that will help. Sal, can you get Ben some paper and a pen?" Garret's voice changed to a whisper along her skin. "Shay?"

She opened her eyes. Garret. Right in her face-space. He was gorgeous and so close. Too bad there were two of him and her head was squeezed in a vise.

"Are you okay?" That breath floated across her cheek, warming her. So good.

Her eyelids fluttered open and closed. It was the only body part she seemed to have control over at the moment. She couldn't move. She tried, but the signals weren't getting through.

Her eyes popped open, and signals ricocheted all over her body, all at once. Her arm moved. Her hands clenched. And her brain realized that getting hit in the head really sucked.

It ached, it pounded, her brain grew two sizes that day—putting pressure on everything. She swore she was minutes from brain cells oozing out her ears like spiders in arsenic sauce.

"Thank God." Garret ran a hand down the side of her face. Too bad her head hurt too much to appreciate it. "Shay?

"Left." That was her voice. Why didn't it sound like her? She'd said the word. She swore she had.

"What?" Garret looked as confused as she felt.

"He was left-handed."

"Okay. We'll talk about that later."

Voices mixed and melded as more noise descended on the room. "The nurse is here."

"Let her through." Garret stayed by Shay's side as a woman in black scrubs kneeled beside him with a tablet in her hand.

"Hi." The nurse looked at Shay with kind eyes. Why was she looking at Shay? She might be on the floor, but it was no big deal. She'd been through worse.

Shay focused her attention on her legs, her arms, her body. Nothing hurt. Just her head. She raised her hand to her hair. Nothing wet. No blood. Yeah. This was nothing. "Hi?"

"Can you tell me your name?"

"Why?" Shay bent her arms, trying to get her elbows under her. She was so done with this whole lay on the floor thing. A strong hand pressed down on her shoulder. Apparently, she wasn't done with this whole lay on the floor thing. Dammit.

"We need to do an assessment." The nurse kept smiling.

Garret ran his fingers under her chin. "Oh God, honey, you were hit pretty hard."

She must have been hit really hard. She could've sworn Garret just called her honey. When had they moved to pet names? The real testament to her head taking a monumental hit was that she didn't hate it. She kind of liked it.

"What's your name?"

"Shayleigh Washington." Shit. Why did she use her whole name?

"Shayleigh?" Garret must be dumber than he looked, questioning her name at a time like this. Hopefully, her glare expressed just how bad an idea that was.

The nurse tapped her fingers on the tablet. "Do you know where you are?"

"Pura Vida hotel in Vegas."

"Perfect." She put down the tablet and produced a small flashlight from somewhere. "Can you sit up?"

Garret helped Shay to a sitting position. A vise wrapped around her brain. Her head swum.

The nurse held up the light. "Follow the light with your eyes."

Shay's eyes moved back and forth. No pain. Nothing. She was fine.

The nurse continued to blind Shay, peering into her eyes. "Good. Why are you here in Vegas?"

"We brought the jewelry for the country music

thing."

She nodded and looked at Garret. "What's the ETA on the ambulance?"

"Wait. What? Did I get one of those wrong?" Shay went through her answers. She was Shay, in Vegas and they came here for the country thing. That's three for three.

"No. You answered correctly. I just want to see how long till the ambulance gets here." The nurse smiled warmly.

"I don't need an ambulance. I'm fine." Shay tried to stand up, but Garret's hand held her down. *Jerk.*

"Hotel policy," he practically grunted.

"I'm sorry. We need you to go to the hospital. Your eyes aren't dilated, but you could still have internal injuries. They'll run a quick CT scan, and you'll be good to go." The nurse was so chipper she actually sounded like she believed what she was saying.

We need you to go to the hospital. Terror balled in Shay's throat as she tried to speak. "I can't go to the hospital." Her voice was raspy and weak. But she had to make him understand.

Shay didn't do hospitals. Not since her parents. Not since she watched her mother die.

"It's policy."

Embarrassment heated her cheeks. She hated to do this, but she wasn't above begging. Not for this. "Please Garret. I can't go." She wrapped her hand around his.

His movements stopped as he stared at her. Maybe he was understanding. Maybe he wouldn't have questions. Maybe she could just go to bed and sleep it off.

"Why?"

She should've known he'd have questions. "I just can't." She stared into his eyes, letting them do all the pleading. Everything about the hospital would destroy her—and nothing that happened in a hospital was ever quick. More like slow and torturous.

"They're here." Sal talked into a mouthpiece, directing the EMTs where to go.

"Can't they clear me?" Shay asked when Garret went to the door and let the EMTs in the room.

A man and a woman came in, each carrying a bag. They played the same games she'd played with the nice nurse a minute ago. Stupid questions. Blinding light.

Surprise, no change. She was fine. The woman went out into the hall and came back with a gurney. Oh hell no.

"Change of plans." Garret poked at his phone. "She's going to the urgent care on Polaris."

The woman looked at Garret like he'd sprouted two noses. "But they might not have everything she needs."

"They're ready for her. They can handle it." He reached for Shay's hand and she took it. An urgent care. It was like a doctor's office. She'd practically lived in doctor's offices and convenient cares back in Chicago, thanks to her gran. Her breathing stuttered back to normal as the panic slowly loosened in her throat. Urgent care was doable. Didn't mean she wanted to do it.

"Do you need us to help you on?" the male EMT asked.

"No." *I don't need help. I'm not getting on.*

"When was the last time you went to the doctor?" Garret leaned toward her.

"A few months ago. Why?"

"So you can handle a trip to urgent care."

"But..."

He patted her back and warm breath tickled her neck. "You're going on that thing."

He set his other hand on her hip, sliding it along her side as his breath tickled her neck again. She wanted to lean back and soak him up—just rest her body against his, maybe get lost in his arms, in his hands. His voice was soft, only for her. "It's policy. And if you don't go willingly, I'd be happy to help you. By any means necessary."

He was being a total jerk and she should be pissed. So why she found her body clenching and her heart racing, she had no clue.

"I've got it." She breathed out on a sigh. She needed to get far away from him. He made her winded like a middle-aged drug dealer running from the DEA.

Shay sat on the gurney and let the EMTs get her settled. Brook came up and wrapped an arm around her. Again, not necessarily a bad thing. It was good to have someone there—someone to lean on. Shay was so damn tired.

"I was so worried about you." Brook wiped her eyes and smiled at Allison, who was standing nearby. "Do you mind if we go with you to the hospital?"

"We're going to urgent care." Shay rolled her head on the pillow to look across the room at Julie. "What about Julie?"

"She'll be right behind you. There's another ambulance on the way." Garret smiled and didn't say the words. He didn't have to. She knew what he was thinking—*hotel policy.*

Garret's breath skated along her skin as he leaned in. His scent surrounded her. Everything about him surrounded her. "We'll talk tomorrow."

His breath disappeared and he was gone. But he'd be back tomorrow. To talk. Probably about today. Great.

She didn't want to think about what the hell she was going to tell Garret about today. She didn't want to talk about her irrational fear of hospitals. And she didn't want to sit at urgent care for the next few hours with nothing to do but think about all of that. All she wanted was some sleep. Like that would happen with the thought of his mouth near her and the possibility of that mouth coming near her tomorrow.

"Shay?" Allison said.

Shay cringed when Allison touched her hand. She must have gotten few good punches in there. Her hand was swollen and torn at the knuckles. She was aching pretty bad, but nothing she couldn't handle.

"I'm so sorry." Allison seemed to be trying to hold back tears.

"We should head out." The EMT kicked the lock on the gurney. "Let's get you checked out so we can get you some pain meds."

Pain meds. She forgot about those. Maybe sleeping tonight wouldn't be so difficult.

CHAPTER ELEVEN

GARRET DRANK deep from his third grande latte of the evening. *Wait.* If it was five thirty in the morning, was it still considered evening? What if you never got a chance to go to bed?

"Okay, so he came in a side door off the Strip," Garret said, more to himself than to Lopez. "He climbed up the south stairs and walked down the hallway." Thankfully, there wasn't much happening on the floor and he was able to monopolize most of the screens in the security office. "Let's move to the outside cameras."

"Please tell me we don't have another fifteen cameras to go through." Lopez drank down his third or fourth coffee.

Another fifteen? There were over fifty cameras lining the outdoors, and depending on which way the guy took, that was how many cameras they'd have to look through.

It had been a long night so far, and there wasn't any

end in sight. After Shay left for the hospital, they'd worked with the cops for a few more hours and then it was video time.

And it had been video time ever since. They'd watched the cameras covering Shay's floor, found the stairway he'd used and fast-forwarded through the main floor till they found how he got in.

They needed to see where he came from. Maybe he didn't have his mask on when he walked in, or maybe, just maybe, he was dumb enough to drive his car into the parking lot. Anything that might lead Garret to this son of a bitch.

He was going to find this guy. And this asshole was going to pay. Seeing Shay on the ground, not moving.? He had been scared to death. He'd thought he'd lost her —not that she was his to lose, but dammit, he didn't want her disappearing.

It nearly killed him, and he wasn't going to let anything happen to her again. Her friends had the same focused dedication. They all sat in front of the screens with Sal and Garret, piecing together the route this asshole had taken.

Shay would have obviously loved to be included, but after the shock of last night, not to mention the pain she was in, she couldn't have stayed up all night. Not like this. She needed her rest. She needed to let her body get past all the pain. Once she was ready, they'd show her the tapes and let her join in, but only if she was feeling well enough.

"Any idea about the tattoo?" Perretti leaned back in

the chair and rubbed his eyes. They needed to wrap this up soon. They were walking dead.

Garret pulled out a crappy drawing of the bear tattoo Mooring mentioned was on the asshole's arm. Julie said it looked familiar, but she had no idea why. And who knew, maybe it was just that the sword was in pretty much every goddamn tattoo out there. Maybe they'd catch a break with the growling bear.

"I've got nothing," Garret said. "I can reach out to a few local tattoo artists. They might have a suggestion of who did the work. If it was even done here in Vegas."

"All right, there are a few different ways a person can get to the side door." Sal fiddled with the mouse and a picture took over the main screen. "Camera one-sixty-five covers the most used route. Let's start there."

They watched a guy pick his nose and wipe it on the outside wall. Garret wrote a note to call house-keeping.

Empty sidewalk. Empty sidewalk.

A woman tripped over her shoes, her dress lifting over her head as she hit the ground. Bonus, she wasn't wearing any underwear. She pulled her dress down and laughed as her friends tried to pick her off the pavement.

A half hour later, the drunk chick with the skirt malfunction was long gone, but there they all were, still staring at footage from the cameras. So much nothing-ness. And yet they watched. They didn't have a choice.

"Wait. That's him." Thank the Lord. "Sal, rewind that." Sal started it again, and Garret jabbed a finger at the screen. "See how he's coming around that wall."

Dammit. He was wearing the damn mask. They were going to need to find the next camera.

Sal grunted. "That leads to the main parking garage. What do you think, camera seventeen?"

"Yeah. That should tell us if he came from the elevator or stairs."

Sal switched cameras, and Garret leaned forward. There weren't many people in the garage. And here the guy was, getting out of the elevator wearing that damn ski mask.

They traced the guy's movements backward, but it was more of the same. Getting into the elevator? Ski mask. Walking to the elevator—two cameras—ski mask.

The guy got out of a blue full-size sedan with the ski mask. No fucking plates. He was officially pissing Garret off. The worst part was this was the exact MO as the jewelry thief that had annoyed the shit out of the Las Vegas PD for the past few months.

Blue full-size sedan.

No plates.

Black ski mask.

There was no reason to believe that this was related to those heists. No fucking reason. "Son of a bitch," Garret swore.

Sal understood. He tossed his pen on the control panel. "Shit."

"Did we miss something?" Byrnes watched from a chair across the room.

"No." Garret leaned his hands on the panel and sighed. "This guy is wanted for a string of jewelry heists in the area. He wears the mask when he drives up. No plates. The car is registered to a ghost—guy died ten years ago. No known relatives. There's no point going through any more videos."

"Cops have been desperate to crack this for months." Sal looked over at Garret, and Garret could practically read his mind. When he nodded, Sal went into Garret's office and got the file that the Las Vegas Metropolitan Police Department was circulating. When Sal told him Metro was desperate, he wasn't lying. They'd sent everything they had to the casinos— well, probably not everything. But it was pretty damn unusual for the cops to keep all the casinos in the loop on something like this.

"All right. I need to tap out." Lopez laid his head back and huffed.

Byrnes opened the file and sifted through the pages. "Yeah, we need to take a few hours and then start up again. Let's meet back here at eleven. That'll give us a good four hours of sleep."

"Yeah." Perretti twisted his neck and got up.

"You guys don't have the security cards to get in this office. I'll meet you upstairs at your room. Eleven?" Garret walked over to the door.

"Yeah." Byrnes closed the file in his hand as he got up from the chair. "Can I take this with? Bedtime reading."

"Sure, but don't let it leave your room." Garret opened the door and led the Chicago's finest out into the hall and up to the casino. "See you."

Heading to the condo side of the property, Garrett thanked God he'd had the foresight to purchase here and not buy a house in Henderson. He'd been tempted. It would have given him a chance to get away at night. But his nights could get pretty long, and a commute would get pretty old.

His five-minute walk was just what he needed at night, and then he could relax with takeout and some Netflix.

Today his walk was in the orange light of morning. It would be beautiful, the sky was amazing first thing in the desert, but he could barely keep his eyes open. He needed to take those four hours and sleep before they hit this thing full power again.

This guy was out there, and he knew where Shay's room was. Garret would take a few hours to make sure he was at the top of his game, but later today he was going to find this creep and make him wish he'd never set foot in Garret's hotel.

CHAPTER TWELVE

THE NEXT DAY, Shay sat in a plush white chair in her hotel room as the doctor pumped up the blood pressure cuff. Really? They could point a nub at her head and find out her temperature, but the best way to figure out the pressure of her blood was by squeezing the life out of her arm.

Angry tingling slowly dissipated from her fingers as the doctor removed the cuff.

"Looking good." He placed the nub of the thermometer to her head. After a beep he pulled it away. "Normal. How's the head feeling, on a scale from one to ten? One being no pain and ten being unbearable."

Five. "Two." She squinted as he shone a light in her eyes. "Maybe three."

"I'm going to give you some ibuprofen to take the edge off."

"When can I get back to work?" Someone had attacked her, Julie, and Ben. Someone had to pay, and she was the cashier. Ugh. Did she always resort to corny lines when she took hits to the head? That was something she could focus on later, because once the doctor gave her a clean bill of health she was out of here. There was no place for this guy to hide.

"Work? You're on vacation." The doctor must have seen the daggers her eyes were throwing. "Can you work? Yes. Should you? No. I know it's hard, but you're still healing. You need to relax."

"We'll make sure she relaxes."

Shay rolled her eyes. She'd forgot about the peanut gallery on the other side of the room. Allison paced, while Brook and Julie sat staring at her. Shay was almost afraid her head was going to start rotating. Why else would everyone be looking at her like a defective science experiment?

"Can she go out in the sun? Or would that be bad?" Allison stopped pacing to ask the question.

"What about drinking? Can she drink?"

"Can she leave the room?"

"How often should we give her medication?"

"Should she swim?"

Shay waited for one of them to ask if the doctor had a spare helmet she could wear. She might bump her head when getting into the elevator. Although maybe she wasn't allowed to go into the elevator because the movement could be too jarring—according to this over-protective group, anyway.

"Yes, she can leave the room. No drinking. If she goes to the pool, keep her out of the sun." The doctor switched his focus back to Shay. "Swimming is fine, but stay aware of your body. If you experience any light-headedness or dizziness, sit down."

The look of horror on the girls' faces at the words lightheadedness or dizziness was almost comical. Almost, because that meant they were going to hover like drones.

"Please call if you need anything." The doctor handed Shay his card. Apparently he worked at the casino. An in-house doctor. The house call was starting to make sense. Which was good, because urgent care had taken forever last night. Not having to go back was a bonus.

"Thank you. I will."

Someone knocked on the door, and Allison ran to open it.

"Good morning. May I come in?"

Shay knew that voice. She had dreams about that voice. When she came to after the attack that voice was all she'd heard, so she was having trouble deciphering what had been real and what had been a dream.

Garret strode into the room, his suit hugging his body in all the right places. And all his places were pretty damn right. He attempted a smile for the women, but Shay could tell something was off. Had he slept? The luggage he was packing under his eyes was enough for a family of four to enjoy a long-weekend ski trip.

"We're just checking on the patient."

We? Shay angled forward and saw Garret's two followers, Perretti and Byrnes. Great. Bad enough she'd have the estrogen drones hovering, now she'd have the testosterone-triplets all in her business.

"She looks good," the doctor said. "Her tests came back negative, and it doesn't appear that she's had any permanent damage. Today she needs to relax, give her body time to heal."

Wait. What? Were they actually talking about her, in front of her? As in, let's pretend Shay's not in the room? "I'm fine."

"Naturally you're fine, but let's wait till you're even more fine till you start back to work." The doctor smiled.

Was it wrong Shay wanted to rip the smile off his face? This group of people would never let her find the asshole who did this. Hell, they wouldn't even let her out of their sight if the doctor was spewing this "rest" crap. It was one thing telling the women, Shay could work around them, but the guys? They'd be another level of pain-in-the-ass.

The doctor left the room, leaving Shay alone with six mother hens.

"Can I get you anything?"

"Are you okay?"

"How are you feeling?"

"Do you need another pillow?"

"Enough." Shay's head was spinning and about to pop right off her neck—and it wasn't from the break-in. "I'm not an invalid. I'm fine. The doctor said I can go back to work. So that's what I'm doing. Did you check the tapes?" She stood up from the couch. Slowly. She was still a bit off, but nothing that some caffeine and work wouldn't fix. She wobbled—dammit—ever so slightly, but they saw it.

Garret reached out and grabbed her elbow. "Are you okay?" Pity rang in his tone and his eyes.

Shay didn't do pity. She yanked her arm away and glared at his hand. Where was her Taser when she needed it? "I'm fine. What was on the tapes?"

"Shay." Perretti blocked the way to her suitcase. "We have this covered. We're still figuring some things out. Just take some time and relax. The girls are going to the pool. Go. Enjoy your vacation."

"The girls?" Shay had busted her ass forward and backward over the years to not be thought of as one of the girls. She'd made sure she could hold her own with men. Generally, women could out-think men, but all it took was for a few women to wimp out when it came to confrontation or fighting—and then all women were weak. Her fingers curled into fists. She wasn't about to lay down now because of a bump on the head.

"Come on, Shay," Joe said. "Don't get all girl-power with me. We've been partners for how long? And I have never once questioned your abilities. You can kick every one of our asses while you out-think us. But you've been hurt. You need to take care of yourself."

"But—"

"If that was me, if I had been hurt, would you let me run around the city? Or would you be nagging the shit out of me to take a break?" Perretti sat down on the couch and pulled her down next to him. "Just one day. Let us track down the leads we've got and give you something to work with tomorrow."

"Fine." She sounded like her brother, all belligerent teen, but Joe was right. If this had happened to him, she'd be all over him to take a day off. Especially since her head was still a bit fuzzy—not that they knew that, but still. "I'll stay here, but when I'm feeling better I expect to be brought up to speed."

Perretti stood up, smiling, and gave her a salute as he walked out the door. Byrnes and Garret waved as they lemminged their way after him.

"Pool time!" Julie danced around the room. "Woot! Woot! Get your suits on, and let's get this party started."

Apparently, the attack last night had put Julie in a good mood. People dealt with stress in interesting and different ways. Which meant it was time to put on a bathing suit.

***

TWO HOURS LATER, Shay sat on the makeshift beach under a poolside cabana. The hot Vegas air mixed with the salty chlorine tickled her nose. Not that it was altogether unpleasant. The pool at the Pura Vida was ridiculous.

The main pool itself was big enough for the two Olympic swim teams to hold trials. And on the far side by the building was a fifty-foot waterfall. It was huge on a grand scale.

Julie splashed around in the shallow end with Brook while Allison sat next to Shay.

"You can go in the pool. You don't have to babysit

me." Shay dropped her phone by her side. If she looked at one more level of Candy Crush, her eyes might bug out.

"I don't want to." Allison turned the page of her *Brides* magazine. "You could go in if you'd like."

"No thanks." Shay would love to jump in the pool, but the women wouldn't let her sit alone on the deck. If she actually got in the pool, they'd probably surround her with open arms in case she tripped. Which was sweet. And annoying.

Shay rested her head against the back of the lounge chair. The sounds of water splashing, people talking, and the rustle of *Brides* magazine was calming. She thought about falling asleep, but her brain just wouldn't turn off long enough to let her.

Splash. Laughter. Rustle. The rhythm soothed her head until the rustling stopped. Shay lifted her head to see if Allison had fallen asleep. Allison stared at her. Just stared, with a tear in her eye.

"Ummm...are you okay?"

Allison smiled. "I'm okay. Thank you for coming with this weekend. I'm so glad you're here." Her smile turned down. "I just wish you hadn't been hurt. It's all my fault."

"Why? You didn't do anything to me."

"I get that. But this is supposed to be a celebration of my marriage, and now it's not. I hate that someone hurt you. I hate that Julie was scared."

"Grab me another Peach Schnapps," Julie called from a raft in the center of the pool. Brook wrapped a towel around her waist and headed to the bar on the other end of the make-shift beach.

"Yeah, Julie looks broken up about last night."

Allison laughed. "You know what I mean. It's a dark cloud over everything. The guys should be here getting us drinks and catering to our whims, not out solving a crime."

"How are you women doing?" Ben walked up to the cabana and sat down. His eyes roamed the resort. Wonder who he was looking for? You could see when he found them because his eyes lit up. Brook was leaning over the side of the pool talking to Julie.

"We're just fine." Allison grabbed his hand. "How are you? Any problems since..." She couldn't even seem to finish the sentence. She was taking the theft harder than anyone.

"I'm fine." He smiled and glanced in her direction. "I wanted to see how Shay and Julie were holding up."

"I'm fine." Not that Ben really cared how she was doing. Well, he probably did. But he didn't care half as much as how Julie was doing. And that was okay. He had it pretty bad for her.

Julie came up the stairs and out of the pool, wrapping a towel, from the stack lining the towel station, around herself as she walked to the cabana. She must not have seen Ben, because if she had she wouldn't be so willing to come this way.

"What's our room number again? Brook is getting us drinks but we can't remember what room we're in..." She stopped when her eyes found Ben.

"Hi, Julie."

"Ben." Julie checked the lounge chair she'd used prior to her swimming excursion and picked up her phone. "He texted." Smiling, she tapped on the screen before showing it to Allison. "He wants to go out tonight." She bounced on the balls of her feet. Julie had lost a bunch of weight, which was awesome, but no one told her chest. So every bounce shoved the goodies in Ben's face.

Poor guy.

"Who texted?" Ben's voice had gone dark. Angry.

"Not that it is any of your business, but I met a guy last night. And he wants to see me again."

The look on Ben's face was more than Shay could take. She swore she saw the moment the poor guy's heart actually broke in half. His face pinched, he tried to smile. "I should get back to the marketing figures."

"Ben." Allison dropped her magazine. "I'll walk with you."

Ben and Allison made their way across the sandy beach and into the hotel. Julie, who was so happy just a minute ago, looked like someone stole her cell phone.

"Where'd Allison go?" Brook walked up with drinks. She set a soda next to Shay and a margarita next to Allison's chair. "I hope I said the right room, otherwise I just charged fifty dollars' worth of drinks to some unsuspecting soul."

Julie grabbed hers and downed the whole glass. Then she entered something into her phone and dropped it on the lounge chair.

"Did you tell him no?" Shay could tell the whole dating thing was killing Julie. She didn't want to date

Muscle 2.0. She wanted to date Ben. Why couldn't she just see it?

"Why would I tell him no?" Julie grabbed Allison's old drink and took a sip. Or two. "He's gorgeous. He's nice. And he wants to go out with me. He hasn't called me a whore or thrown my stuff down the stairs. He hasn't kicked me out of his house or completely abandoned me without a word."

Another sip. Or was that a gulp?

"He doesn't think I'm so replaceable that he can just disappear into thin air."

And now onto Allison's new drink.

"Disappear for about a year. One year with no contact. Do I know if he's hurt? Dead in a ditch? Nope. I'm just supposed to not care. Like he does. But I'm not like that. I have a heart. I can't turn off the emotions like some sociopathic jackass." She emptied Allison's glass and flopped onto the chair.

Brook sat next to her and wrapped an arm around her. Julie's shoulders shook as tears fell down her face. Shay and Brook looked at each other. Neither knowing what the hell to do. Emotions and tears were Allison's area of expertise. The three of them sat there like that for a few minutes—or a few hours, it was pretty much the same. Uncomfortable and awful.

"Look at me." Julie ran a hand over her face. "Blubbering like a fool. Let's go for a swim." She wobbled to her feet. "You coming?" she asked as she waded into the pool and grabbed a floaty.

Brook looked over to Shay. "Coming?"

"Nah, I'm going to head up to the room. Get out of the heat for a bit."

"Do you want me to come with?"

"No, go swim. I'll see you later." Shay'd had enough of the hot weather and the drama. She was bored out of her mind. She couldn't play another game on her phone. She couldn't read another vapid magazine. Her head didn't spin. Her body felt good enough to move about.

It was time to get back to work.

CHAPTER THIRTEEN

THE SUN BEAT down on Garrett's face after they got out of his car and entered another tattoo shop. He'd never truly thought about how many tattoo places were within a mile of the Strip until now. They had to keep looking till they found the one that could have done that tattoo. The snarly-looking bear with the medieval sword. Didn't make sense why anyone would put those two things together. But apparently someone had. Then again, half the people that came through the security office did crazy shit that he could never in a million years understand.

The guy who stuck his erection in the mouth of a Snapple bottle because his friends dared him to? Garret didn't get it. That the same guy broke said Snapple bottle because he couldn't get his manhood out—still confusing. That when the top ring of the bottle wouldn't come off, the guy used a pen to break it and ended up with glass lodged in his penis? Nope.

The fact that Garret ended up sitting with the idiot

and his drunk friends at the hospital—nope. That night had not been one of his favorites. It was early in his career, and he'd been inches away from quitting back then, but Maria had wanted to get a house together, and there wasn't anything he wouldn't have done for her. So he'd stuck it out and slowly rose through the ranks.

Not that it was all for her. He didn't regret sticking with his job. After she'd left, it had been the best thing he had going in his life. Hell, it still was.

He followed Perretti, Lopez, and Byrnes into the Devil's Cut. Graphic art of blood, skulls and boobs covered the dark wood walls. Wow. A lot of boobs. Seemed to be a popular theme—not that Garret understood that either.

But who was he to judge? He wasn't exactly following the logical path these days. The Vegas PD had told him to stay out of this investigation. They told him they'd look into the attack. But something primal in Garret wouldn't let him do that. He didn't see the harm in poking around to see if they could find the guy with the tattoo. So he was wandering around Vegas with a few Chicago cops most definitely not staying out of the investigation.

After all, Vegas PD was hammered—too many cases, not enough cops. And here Garret had three cops at his disposal... or really four cops, but he'd never presume to have Shay at his disposal. The woman would eat him for lunch if he even harbored that thought.

"Hey." Garret walked up to the front counter and

pulled out the rough sketch of the tattoo. "Could anyone in this shop have done this?"

"Doubtful." The young guy behind the counter glanced at the paper and shook his head. "That's not even close to what we do here, man."

"Hey, handsome." A woman with studs in her nose and her ears and probably other places walked up to the counter. Her tight T-shirt and tight jeans showed some impressive assets. Almost made Garret want to see what other body parts were pierced. But all he could think about was Shay and the asshole who touched her.

"Wow, a bunch of handsomes. Is there a hot guy convention in town?" She pretended to fan herself as she walked around the counter and held out a well-manicured hand. "Sharyl."

Garret shook, hell, they all shook her hand. She was a friendly little thing. "So, what kind of ink are you looking for? Maybe a group tat to remember your trip to Sin City. Something manly, maybe a snake—no, a really long python."

"No thanks. Actually, we have some questions." Garret handed her the sketch. "Could anyone in this shop or anyone you know have done this tattoo?"

She looked at the paper and laughed. "The Aussies with Flossies tat? Nah, no one here does the muscled studs. Although, I could think of some things I'd like to do to them—a tattoo is only one of them—and not at the top of my list."

"The Aussies with what?" Lopez inched his way toward Sharyl.

"Aussies with Flossies. You know, the Profane from Brisbane—that show at the Blink. Most of the guys get this tattoo in solidarity or whatever."

"Is there one specific place they go?"

She shook her head. "Not really. It's more a question of who than where. I know Walter does these. He works out of the shop on Paradise. Right by Hard Rock. Bogey retired. Umm..." She traced a finger over the sketch. "I'm not sure who else is doing them these days."

"Thanks." It wasn't much, but it was more than they'd gotten so far.

She handed the paper back to him. "Anything else? You look like you need some ink."

"I'm good." Garret folded the picture and slid it in his pocket.

The four of them headed out into the Vegas sun and on to the next tattoo shop. Fifteen minutes and an uneventful view of Paradise Road later, they stood in front of Voltage Tattoos. Byrnes and Lopez spotted a McDonald's down the block and offered to grab some coffee to get through the rest of the day. Garret didn't argue. The almost four hours he'd slept wasn't cutting it.

Perretti opened the glass door to the tattoo parlor, and he and Garret made their way up to the counter. The shop was buzzing. Literally. Between the pauses in heavy metal music, the buzzing of the tattoo machines came through loud and clear.

The room was wide open. People sat in black recliners, and the artists leaned over them, completely focused. Framed tattoo art hung along the wall by the front counter, and a giant TV dominated the far wall. The place was immaculate. Loud, but immaculate.

"Hey, guys. What can I do for you?" A young guy in a Black Sabbath tee came up behind the counter.

"We were hoping to talk to one of your artists. Is Walter in?"

"Yeah, he's with a client right now." Black Sabbath glanced at one of the chairs under the big screen. "He's got another hour or two."

"Is there any way we can talk to him for a minute during a break or something?" Perretti pulled one of Walter's cards from a holder on the counter.

"One minute." Black Sabbath walked over by the television and got the attention of one of the artists. There were words, although Garret couldn't hear any of them over the noise. There was nodding, which was a good sign.

The guy in the chair smiled and stood up, stretching his arms over his head. Even from here Garret could see the ink on the guy's leg. Bright. Vivid. It truly was an art form.

"Hi, I'm Walter." A short guy with a beard pulled off his nitrile gloves and smiled. "What can I do for you?" he asked, offering Garret his hand.

Garret shook it and pulled out the picture. "I'm Garret. I work over at Pura Vida. I was told you might be able to help me. Have you done any tattoos for the guys from the Profane from Brisbane show?"

Walter frowned. "I've done a few of them. Is something going on?"

"How many of these tattoos have you've done?" Perretti asked.

"Fifty. Seventy-five." Walter shrugged. "A shit-ton."

"Is there any way we can get a list of people who have gotten this tattoo?"

"We don't generally give out client information. That's against our policy. Sorry." Walter did look sorry, not that it helped Garret right about now.

"I get it," Garret said, thinking fast. "But can you tell me if you've done this tattoo on anyone outside of employees of the Profane from Brisbane show?"

Walter nodded. "I can answer that. No. Only employees get it. Mostly dancers."

"So other employees can get it as well."

"Sure. I've done a producer, a manager, some road-ies, security. You name it, they've been through here. Can I ask you something?" Walter continued when Garret nodded. "Is this something I need to be concerned with?"

"I don't think so." Garret smiled. "Thanks for the information. Tell that guy thanks for letting us take up his time."

Walter stretched his arm across his chest. "It's all good. We were a few minutes from a break anyway. It's rough, sitting in one position for six hours. That's why we split up the big ones into multiple days."

Six hours. Multiple days. Garret wasn't sure he could handle one hour, let alone six—more than once. No wonder everyone was always so proud of their ink, especially when it looked good. It took dedication to sit for it, and if you picked the right tattooist, it was a work of art.

"Here's my card if you have any other questions."

"Thanks, man." Garret took the card and nodded to Walter.

Outside, Garret and Perretti found Lopez and Byrnes leaning against the car. They were sucking down caffeine like toddlers with chocolate shakes.

"Get what we need?" Byrnes handed over two large coffees.

Perretti took a long pull. "Sort of. The tats aren't just for the dancers, they're for the staff too."

"Interesting. So, we heading to the Aussies with Flossies?" Byrnes pulled away from the car and laughed. "That cracks me up."

Garret looked at his watch. It was only two o'clock, and the show wasn't until later tonight. There might not be a lot of people, but it was still worth checking out. "Yeah, let's go."

They piled into Garret's SUV. Again. Garret navigated the streets. Again. It felt like he'd been driving for days. He couldn't wait to get this guy. Once Shay was safe, he was going to spend a long time in bed.

And he couldn't even find the energy to think of how much he wanted Shay in that bed and all the things he'd like to do to her. Okay, he could find the energy for that. He couldn't help it. He really liked her. Her strength. Her intelligence. Her beauty. He liked that she spoke her mind. Too many women didn't say what they really wanted, they just walked away.

She was the full package. And he couldn't stand that the package was in danger.

———

SHAY WAS DRESSED AND CLEAN, after a steaming hot shower to scrub the desert air and sand from her skin. Being clean didn't make her feel any less dirty, however. She'd followed an employee with a key card from the main floor to the dark back hallways and through the secured area of the building. She shouldn't be here, but so far no one had noticed her sneaking behind the scenes, which meant she was currently standing in front of the security doors of Pura Vida.

Hopefully, the guys wouldn't give her a hard time about starting work so soon, or piggybacking on a card-carrying employee—a total no-no, she was sure. But she was desperate. She couldn't do it anymore. She'd sat by the pool like a good little patient. But a patient patient she was not. If she sat at that pool one more minute, she might lose her mind or her will to live.

She knocked on the door and held her breath. She didn't want to fight. She just wanted to keep busy. The door flung open. Rick stood there. A scowl, then a smile aimed right at Shay. "Hey, how are you feeling?"

She wasn't sure what to say. There was no reason to tell him about any of the doctor stuff or how she was doing. She just wanted to see the files. Maybe get a look at the videos.

"I'm good. Garret left the files down here for me. The files on my attack." She knew what to say. Push the truth a bit, or... Oh, who was she kidding? She was flat-out lying. Desperate times and all.

"Yeah." He looked uncertain. Shit. He must know she was told to take the day off. She needed to cut this off now.

"The doctor said I'm ready to work."

"Oh, good." He worried his lip between his teeth—which was adorable, but not the response she was looking for. "I'm not sure if I can let you back here."

"Really? Why?" Shay pulled out her best smile. The one that her slimy two-timing husband called her penis-tamer. Whenever she used that smile on him, he'd bend to her will...until a girl half his age lured him in with her version of the penis-tamer and destroyed their marriage.

Needless to say, Shay didn't use this particular superpower all that often. Who wanted a guy who could be controlled with a simple smile? On the other hand, Rick was different. She wasn't looking for a relationship here. She just needed information—information about herself. It was rightfully hers. Yeah. That was her story.

"Policy. Only Garret can let people back here."

"Oh." The word deflated in her chest. You didn't become Lieutenant without a firm grasp of policy, and she wasn't about to let this guy get in trouble because of her. "Could you bring the files out to me? You could do that, right?"

Rick nodded with his own "tamer" of a smile. He disappeared behind the door and a moment later came out with the file. He held it out, and as she reached for the folder, he pulled it back. "So, if you're feeling good enough to work, you should be well enough for dinner. Will you go out with me?"

"I am." She felt absolutely fine. And maybe dinner could be fun. She held out her hand for the folder. He was holding it hostage. Shit. "Well, I should take that and start the investigation."

"I'm waiting on your answer?"

"If I say no will you not hand it over?" The edge in her voice matched the edge in her body.

He sighed and handed her the file. "No. I just like you. I thought you might want to go out for dinner. See some of the local hangouts."

Her mind raced, looking for a reason to say no. Garret would hate if she had dinner with this guy. Or maybe he wouldn't. Maybe she wanted him to hate if she had dinner with another man.

But he was just some guy she'd kissed. Garret meant nothing. So why wasn't she saying yes to dinner?

"Dinner could be nice." It was only dinner. One dinner. So what if she'd rather have dinner with Garret. Didn't mean she couldn't go out and have a simply lovely time with this guy.

"Really? Great. How about tonight, seven o'clock?"

"See you then." She tried to make her voice sound half as excited as she should feel. Why she wasn't that excited wasn't something she wanted to dwell on.

She thanked him and headed back to the casino floor. It took every ounce of restraint not to whip open the file folder and start reading right here, but doing that in the middle of vacationers and gamblers wasn't a good idea.

She walked along the bright blue carpet until she found Starbucks. Okay, so it really wasn't private or secure, but they had some damn good coffee. And no fact-finding mission was ever complete without caffeine.

She ordered an espresso macchiato and a piece of pound cake—because no fact-finding mission was ever complete without pound cake, either—and found a booth in the back.

Opening the file, she pulled out detailed accounts and pictures of her injuries. She'd been there, felt that. Next.

Julie's injuries—bump to the head, cut along her arm. Nothing out of the ordinary. Nothing that said what angle the guy would have been hitting her from, indicating his height. Ben's injuries weren't any more telling.

The guy wore gloves, according to Ben. Shay barely remembered that. What did she remember? Before she looked farther down Ben's statement, maybe she should seriously think about the guy...

She closed her eyes. He was tall with a broad chest. Definitely a man. What did he wear? All black. Black hoodie. Black mask. Black pants. Black shoes. Dark eyes? Maybe. Left-handed. Nothing else. She couldn't see anything else.

She opened her eyes and checked Ben's statement. No surprise, it was the same description she just gave— almost word for word. *Black hoodie. Black ski mask.*

Black sweatpants. Pretty damn close, considering she'd been knocked on her ass.

Ben had a few more details. *When the perp was fighting with Shay, his sleeve pulled up. White skin with a tattoo on his arm of black bear-looking thing with round ears, teeth were showing and a giant sword handle crossed its chest...*

The tattoo sounded familiar. She flipped through the pages to the artist's drawing. *Holy crap.* She knew that tattoo. She'd watched that tattoo twirl around her friend on stage *Magic Mike* style.

Did she mention holy crap?

She sifted through the rest of the file. A whole lot of nothing—except the drawing of the tattoo. That was not nothing. It seemed she was going on a little excursion back to Profane from Brisbane theatre. She had to find Muscles One and find out what exactly he'd done after he left the stage last night.

CHAPTER FOURTEEN

SHAY WALKED through the Blink Hotel casino, past the giant fiberglass kangaroo and the plastic koala hanging from the center of the arched doorway. The lobby of the theatre was empty, except for a bartender surrounded by boxes in front of the main bar.

"Hello." Shay approached the man as he lifted bottles of vodka out of the box.

"We're not open yet." He put the bottles on the bar. The scowl on his face didn't change. Although it might have grown a little deeper as he watched her.

"I need to see..." Muscles One? What the hell was his real name? They'd announced it overhead last night. Too bad, she was too busy bachelorette-partying to remember. She should have been better prepared. Take the girl out of Chicago and somehow you took the cop out of the girl.

"See what?" He took an empty box and tossed it to the ground before kicking it. What a charmer. He must be saving all of the flirty-niceness that Shay had seen the night before for later. Jerk.

Improvise. She pulled out her badge. "I need to see a manager."

"Kat's in the back office. Through there." He nodded at a set of double doors next to the stage. Didn't offer to walk her back. Didn't even lift a finger to point. Just a nod and scowl and go the fuck away.

Okay, he didn't say that, but he might as well have.

"Thanks." She didn't want to say it, but her Gran always did say to kill them with kindness unless it's easier to just kill them. She'd kill him, but this guy wasn't worth catching a case. He returned to his boxes of booze, didn't acknowledge her at all. Not worth it.

She walked through the darkened room, and the place lost some of the booze and smoke smell. Today, in the light of day, it smelled like bleach and booze and smoke. Interesting combination.

She pushed through the doors. She didn't know what she expected to see, but maybe a hallway or something. Instead, she was looking at lockers. The guys' lockers. Holy crap. Thank goodness she was wandering around during the day. Heaven knew what she would walk in on during one of their shows.

Although, the men with big muscles and gorgeous smiles bending over and taking off their shoes could be interesting...

"Who are you, and what are you doing back here?" A woman in a black pantsuit and stocking feet walked out of a shoe-box office.

"I'm Detective Washington." Shay flashed her badge.

"Is there a problem?"

"Not at all. Do you have time for a few questions, Ms....?"

"Katrina Drake, but you can call me Kat." The woman glanced down at her feet. "Do I need to wear shoes?"

"Not for me."

"Then I have all the time in the world." Kat motioned to a bench by the lockers. "Have a seat. The guys won't be in for a few hours."

Shay sat on the bench across from Kat. She pulled out a hotel notepad and pen from her pocket. Tools of the trade. "I'm trying to find one of your dancers. He pulled the bachelorettes on stage last night."

"What is this about? Is he in trouble?"

Shay took the picture of the tattoo from the back of the notepad and unfolded it. "We're investigating a break-in. We think he might have some information. Does he have this tattoo on his arm?"

Kat nodded at the sheet of paper and smiled. "Him and everyone else. Although some of the guys have it on different body parts." Kat pulled down the collar of her shirt and showed her upper chest, where that stupid bear and sword sprawled across her skin. "I even have one."

"Does everyone have the bear and sword?"

Kat laughed. Deep. Apparently Shay was a comedian.

"It isn't a bear. It's a Tasmanian devil. You know, Australia, Down Under, and all."

That made so much more sense. Made a hell of lot more sense than a teddy bear, anyway.

"The bachelorette dancer last night was Jon. He has the tattoo on his arm."

"Can I get his address?"

"Sorry. We don't give out that type of information without a warrant." At least Kat smiled as she delivered the bad news.

"Can you tell me when he works next?"

"Sure. He'll be here tonight. After five thirty. The show starts at seven, so if you could be here closer to six, I would really appreciate it. I can't have him distracted when he's trying to work."

Shay couldn't help but smile. The woman gave Shay what she wanted. A timeframe. It just meant she had to wait a few hours before she could go any further. "Thank you for your help. I'll be here at six." Shay put the pen and papers back in her pocket as she stood.

"See you then." Kat walked back into her office.

Shay walked through the double doors and across the bar, making sure to wave at the bartender with the lack-of-personality disorder. He scowled. At least he was consistent. When she made it outside, into another sunny Vegas afternoon, she was so blinded that she almost didn't see the large men walking toward her. But she could hear them.

"Why are you here?"

She knew that voice. "Hello, Perretti. Nice to see you, too."

"Seriously, Washington, what are you doing here? Aren't you supposed to be relaxing—drinking mai tais by the pool?" That was Byrnes. Between Perretti, Byrnes, Lopez, and Garret, there was no way she was getting to a taxi without throwing a punch. She didn't want to fight.

"I got bored." She tried to block the sun with her hands. One hand knocked against the sunglasses resting on her head. She pulled them down.

"How did you know to come here?" Garret asked the obvious question. The one she didn't want to answer.

"I thought I'd catch an early show and check out the dancers. You can imagine my disappointment when I got here and found out it wasn't open yet." She added a pout for good measure. The bland look Garret shot her way suggested the pout might have been too much. "Fine. I'm out here doing my job—following clues."

"And where did you find clues to follow at the pool?" Garret looked pissed. Which meant he probably knew exactly where she'd gotten her clues. Hopefully, he didn't know how she'd obtained said clues, though. She didn't think that wouldn't go over really well.

"I got the file and I thought I'd help. Nothing more."

Garret moved closer. "From who?"

If he thought she'd be intimidated, he was sadly mistaken. "Whom."

"Excuse me?"

"From whom?" Okay. So, should she be correcting

his grammar at a time like this? No. Did she regret it? Hell, no. He shouldn't be squaring up with her. He really brought this on himself. Of course, that was little consolation as his face morphed to a barely contained explosion.

He could crumble the Stardust with that one look. "I don't have time for grammar right now."

"There's always time for proper English."

Perretti and Byrnes could barely contain their laughter, while Lopez was so immersed in some text he was writing that he missed all the fun.

Garret's look shifted from barely contained explosion to uncontained. The guy was going to blow a damn gasket.

Fine. "I got the file from your office."

"From Rick." He rolled his eyes when she didn't reply. "I have cameras. I will find out."

FINE. "I got it from Rick." Her tone might have been annoyance with a side of bitchy. Again, his fault. He drove her absolutely insane.

"So you got the file from Rick." His tone told her that Rick would be hearing an earful later.

Sorry, Rick.

"What in the file brought you here? What clues did you follow with your magnifying glass?"

What clues? She knew what clues brought her to this building. What clues brought them here? Sharing was a two-way street or she wasn't driving it. "No."

"No? That wasn't a yes or no question."

"No, I'm not answering. I'm not showing you mine if you're not going to show me yours." She knew how bad that sounded, but it was what came out of her mouth. And it fit.

"Oh, I'll show you mine..." Garret and his thunderous gaze inched forward.

So damn close she could practically taste him. She could smell the mint on his breath, and her body liked it. Was it wrong that the thought of him showing her his got her body all hot and bothered? She could just imagine what his looked like. Num.

Okay, that was wrong. Even she could see that, and she was mid-drool. The guy was being a tool. And she didn't tolerate tools. No matter how hot they were. She propped her hands on her hips. "Look—"

"Shay. How's your head?" Perretti angled between her and Garret. Tried to angle, anyway. They were practically nose to nose. She was so close to reaching out and slapping someone.

"I'm fine." Amazing how she could speak through clenched teeth. Must be all the practice.

"Look." Garret stepped back and ran a hand down the nape of his neck. "We'll tell you how we got here if you tell us. But let's get inside and do a few interviews first."

See, he could learn. "Okay, but the guys aren't in. There was a female manager and a bartender. The rest of the staff will be in later."

"How much later?" Lopez looked up from the small screen. He was actually paying attention, who knew.

"We have about five hours."

"Ohhh. Yeeaah." His fingers flew over the screen.

Shay shook her head. "How is it that you can make regular words sound seedy?"

"It's a gift."

As far as she was concerned, she didn't need Lopez around for the interviews. Especially since it was clear he'd much rather be someplace else. In fact, she could handle the whole damn thing on her own.

"Look, Lopez, go do whatever or whoever you want. We don't all need to be here interviewing." She cut off Byrnes before he started to argue. "In fact, having all of us here will just draw more attention than we need. Garret, don't you have a hotel to run? Byrnes and Perretti, go to your women. I'll take care of things here." Simple. Direct. Now they all just needed to go.

"You're not staying here alone." Garret burst her perfect little alone bubble.

"Why?"

Byrnes dropped a hand on her shoulder. "Sorry, I have to agree. Two is better than one."

Yeah, but that didn't mean she had to like it. Because if there would be two, it wouldn't be her and one of Chicago's finest. No. She wasn't that lucky. They all had someone waiting for them back at the hotel. It would be Garret and his annoying, gorgeous face.

Garret turned toward the guys. "Why don't you head back to the hotel, go see your ladies. Try to salvage some of this vacation. Shay and I will handle the interviews. We can reconvene and compare notes tomorrow." Naturally, that was how it would shake out. Stupid Garret.

"Are you okay with that?" Perretti looked at Shay with such hope. He wanted to go back to Brook and the hotel. He'd be crazy not to.

She didn't have the heart to break his. So she smiled. "Go. Have fun. We got this."

Lopez gave a little whoop and aimed himself toward the taxi queue by the other end of the hotel entrance. "I'm heading back to the hotel now for anyone wanting a ride back." He walked along the sidewalk with Byrnes following close behind.

"Call if you need anything." Perretti nodded and then ran to catch up with the other two. A valet flagged a taxi and the three disappeared, leaving her alone with *him*.

She sighed and turned to Garret. "I was going to hit the Chicago-style pizza place around the corner if you want to come."

He winced. "As a man who's had real Chicago-style, you do not want to go in there. I have a better idea." He pressed the alarm on his key fob and opened the doors.

"Where are we going?" She stared at his SUV. The word warily came to mind.

"Trust me." He smiled as he opened the passenger door, a huge smile spread across his face. Trust him? Hah. It wasn't him who couldn't be trusted.

She was the one who couldn't be alone with him in a car. She was the one who couldn't seem to get her mind out of the gutter when it came to him.

Before she could get inside the SUV, his body invaded her space. He had her pinned to the door.

Oooh, and his body could pin her any day of the week. *See?* This was why he was so dangerous.

He slid a hand down the side of her face, sending little jolts skittering down to her toes. "Are you really okay? I was worried about you."

"I'm feeling better," someone's breathy voice said. *Crap.* It was her.

"Good." His lips found hers. Soft and warm. Those jolts were now giant booms through her center. Slow and languid. Her body pulsed.

He pulled those lips away too soon. "Let's get you some lunch."

She got in the car and laid her head against the seat. She was in so much trouble here. But somehow, as her lips trembled and her blood tingled, she didn't seem to care.

GARRET PULLED out of the hotel parking lot and headed down Las Vegas Boulevard, aka the Strip, toward Sahara Avenue. Most people came to Vegas and never left the Strip, not to sightsee, not to eat. There was a lot to do on the Strip, but there was so much more off-Strip. Great restaurants, museums, off-roading—hell, nature in general awaited anybody who left the commercial fluorescent blaze.

The real Las Vegas was a whole other world that most people rarely saw. He turned into the parking lot of one of his favorite restaurants, Capone's, an Italian joint reminiscent of a speakeasy. He found a parking spot along the side of the plain white brick building. "Ready?"

"Starving." Shay opened her door and jumped out. "I didn't get a chance to eat today."

"Weren't you at the pool all day? Why didn't you eat then?"

She shrugged, glanced at the blank wall of the building, and headed around the side. He leaned against his car and waited until she came back. "Where's the door?" she asked, scowling.

He smiled and led her around the other way, opening the door for her and following her through.

Inside the vestibule were four walls. No doors, just a pay phone hanging on one wall. Did he mention this was reminiscent of a speakeasy? It was small, which meant he was standing close to Shay. So close he could smell apricot on her skin.

He almost closed his eyes and took a deep breath—but that would be creepy and weird. He didn't close his eyes. He didn't move, either. He watched as she realized that there was no door.

"What the hell?" She lifted the phone from its cradle. No dial tone. Garret had tried that before. Shay found a small buzzer on the wall and pressed.

A tiny panel opened in the wall, and blue eyes stared at them from the other side. Claudia's voice came through the small opening. "Whaddaya want?"

Yes, Garret knew how sad it was that he knew the greeter personally. He ordered from here that often.

"Garret? What are you doing here during lunch?" Claudia closed the spyhole and whipped open the wall which was really a door. "Shouldn't you be working?"

"I'm off today." He followed Claudia inside the restaurant, guiding Shay with a hand on her back.

The greeter held out a chair for Shay and laid the menus on the table. "Your server will be right with you."

He loved this place and he loved watching Shay take it all in. The restaurant was all dark wood and red leather elegance, with a sleeping black piano sitting in the center of the far wall. *The Godfather* ran in a loop on televisions over the bar.

"I hope you like Italian." Garret pretended to look through the menu. He'd always ordered the same thing.

"Who doesn't love Italian?" She turned over the menu and smiled. "Best meatballs on earth, huh?"

"On earth." He nodded. "The original owner came from Chicago and wanted food that reminded him of back home. I don't think anyone has challenged his meatball claim, yet."

"Who would, with the mob theme?"

"Exactly."

The waiter came up to the table. "Welcome, is this your first time here?"

Shay nodded. Garret said, "No."

"Welcome back." He turned from Garret to Shay. "And we hope you enjoy your meal. What can I get for you?"

Shay glanced at the drink selections. "I'll have whatever beer you have on tap."

Garret couldn't help but smile as he stared at her.

The women he'd dated were never the beer type. They were Dom Perignon and truffles. Which wasn't bad, but this was more his speed. "I'll have the same."

Shay narrowed her eyes at Garret. "Why do you keep looking at me like that?"

"Nothing. You just keep surprising me."

"Garret." A moment later, Claudia walked up to the table carrying their two beers. She must have overheard their order and hurried on over. Which wasn't difficult since the lunch rush was over and only a few locals sat at the bar. "Brenda and I stayed at your hotel last week, but we didn't see you."

"I've been busy planning for the country awards."

"Oh, that's right. How'd it go?"

"Interesting." He left it at that. No one needed to know who was puking in the ficus or making out in the elevators. Although there had been a lot of both of those things. The blackmail material he had, if he ever decided to go to the dark side.

Claudia rested a hand on his shoulder. "I'm sure. Maybe we'll catch you next time."

"Yeah. Give me a heads-up before you stop by, we can grab a drink."

"Absolutely." She squeezed his shoulder and disappeared into the kitchen.

Shay rolled her eyes. "Another adoring fan."

"Fan, no. Friend, yes. Her wife decorated my apartment. She's an incredible interior designer, for the record."

"Oh." Shay took a sip of her beer. "So, how long have you been working in security?"

"Seven years here. Six years with the Navy."

"Why'd you leave?"

He hated that question. The question was innocuous enough, but telling the truth always tore at him. He thought about blowing her off, telling her some BS story about his tour being done and wanting to come back home. But that wasn't entirely true. And he didn't want to lie. Not to her.

The air left his lungs as the words spilled from his lips. "I was in Fallujah setting up the security for a friendly's house. An Iraqi diplomat. There were five of us—three to work on the system, and two guards. It should have been an easy setup, but I had trouble getting one of the cameras to work. The other guys told me to just let it go. There were enough cameras."

He should have listened. Why hadn't he listened when the guys said something was off? Maybe they'd all be here now. "Back then, I would get so involved in the work that I didn't pay attention to anything else. The friendly was jittery, which wasn't like him. Something wasn't right. But I didn't listen to my crew."

Shay slid her hand over his—a balm for the pain of the words he had to say. The admission he had to make. Not many people knew the story. And of those who did, not many understood. "When we were done, we packed up and headed out, and drove straight into an ambush.

"The driver kept going despite being shot in the chest, and he got us to the base. I don't know how he drove the three miles. Grace of God maybe. But when we got back to the base and they transferred him to the gurney, he died. They all did, because I didn't listen."

"That ambush would have been waiting no matter when you left." Her fingers slid along his. "You know that, right? It's not really your fault."

He wanted to believe that, but deep down he knew it wasn't true. "After that, I just couldn't do it anymore. I finished my tour and headed back stateside as soon as I could."

"Is that why you didn't join the police force when you came back?"

Two for two. He hated that question even more. He hated what that implied, that he somehow wasn't good enough to be a cop or that he didn't have any motivation to make something of his life. He got that crap from his ex. But somehow, the question held no judgment in Shay's mouth.

"No. I never thought about becoming a cop. In the Navy, I maintained and installed security equipment. It's harder to find something like that in law enforcement. So, what about you? How long have you been a cop?"

"Twelve years. I'd like to think I started when I was ten." She smiled. Really smiled. She was so damn beautiful.

"Even if you weren't ten, you must have been young."

"I graduated from high school when I was seventeen and got my bachelor's degree in criminal justice. So, I joined the force as soon as I turned twenty-one." She took another pull at her beer as she frowned. "I was always seen as the youngest. The one with the least experience. I had to prove myself. So I did. Sergeant at twenty-six and lieutenant at thirty-two. If I play all the games, I'll be chief by the time I'm forty-five. At least, that's the plan."

Like she'd proved herself at the casino. "You deserve it. You're an incredible detective."

"You've just met me. How can you know?"

"It's hard to miss." He watched her duck her head and he loved that he could have that effect on her. "You were amazing identifying the cheaters at the poker tables. And you were able to keep order the day of the awards. That doesn't even cover the fact that you caught up to our investigation in a couple of hours."

"I didn't do anything special," she mumbled.

"You don't give yourself enough credit. You're a great detective."

"It's the only thing I've ever been good at."

"I find it hard to believe that's the only thing you're good at."

She shrugged and stood. "Excuse me. I need to run to the washroom."

Garret stood, too, and watched her walk away. Even though the words he'd said felt right, he also felt they were somehow wrong.

CHAPTER FIFTEEN

SHAY STARED into the full-length mirror and prayed for a bolt of lightning or a swarm of locusts. Anything would be better than this—this—was it even a date?

No, definitely not a date. A nightmare.

The conversation played back in her mind.

"I find it hard to believe that's the only thing you're good at."

No one other than her gran had ever said anything that nice. And if they did, she sure as hell didn't believe them. But she believed Garret. Heaven help her. Why?

When he was a sexist jerk, she could handle him. She could ignore him—sort of. She could at least pretend she wasn't interested.

But dammit. Those green eyes and those perfect teeth. Ugh. He wasn't her type, but he was so nice to look at. And nice. And those hands. His hands were big and they felt great along her skin. Just the memory made her body pulse in inappropriate places.

And it felt good. Too good. It had been a long time

since any part her had quivered without some battery-operated device. Who had time to date, let alone meet someone to get down and dirty with? Between work, her gran, and her brother, there was always something or someone that needed her attention.

This thing that was happening with Garret—no matter how much she didn't want it—it was happening. And she liked it. She hadn't done something just for herself in a long time. And doing Garret would be all about herself.

She was on vacation, and once she left Vegas she would have to join the real world where she was losing everything. Why not use this vacation to gain something? That's what vacation was all about. Find yourself a hot local and take a dip. Ask Lopez…

Things had gotten pretty bad if she was taking her cues from Lopez, the man-whore. He'd rested his piece in more holsters than Smith & Wesson.

She turned on the faucet and ran her hands under the stream. Maybe he had it right. She lived in Chicago. Garret lived in Vegas. They could have their fun and never see each other again.

She flicked her hands and dried them. Yeah, she could do this. She could holster up and scratch that itch and then move on.

It wasn't that hard. She'd just take what she needed and head back home.

She walked out of the bathroom and straight to the table where Garret sat. She couldn't help but smile. He was delicious and this would be fun.

She could totally do this.

GARRET LIKED THIS RESTAURANT, but today was the best lunch he'd had in a long time. "So, tell me something about yourself." He wanted her to talk. He didn't care about what.

"I've told you plenty." Shay shook her head. "It's your turn. Are you married?"

"I was married." He smiled. Ever since she'd gotten back to the table she'd been ready to talk. And he could admit he liked it. Talking about himself...he didn't like.

"Was?"

He might be wrong, but he swore that was relief in her eyes. Too bad this topic didn't give him any relief. "I was married for few years, but it didn't work out. She left."

"Why'd she leave?" Shay had been much more relaxed since she came back from the bathroom. As long as the conversation stayed on him. And even though he hated talking about his past, he wanted her to get to know him.

"I'm not sure."

She raised an eyebrow, like she somehow knew what drove his perfectly happy bride back to Montana.

"One minute she was here, and then she was gone." Which was the truth. He'd come home to find all of her stuff had been removed from the apartment. "She said she wasn't happy."

And she must not have been. Not that she'd ever told him that. He'd had to hear it from her dad when he'd tried to talk to her after she moved back home. He thought they were living the dream. He was building a career, they were talking about buying a house, having a family. His picket fence was so close he could feel the splinters.

And then it was all gone. "What about you?"

"What about me?"

He smiled. The woman was smart enough to know what he meant and stubborn enough to pretend she didn't understand. "Have you ever been married?"

"Once."

He put his fork down and watched her. He wanted her to elaborate, but he wasn't interested in playing a game of twenty questions.

"What?" She sighed and picked up her beer. "Fine. I was married for a few years. Divorced for even more."

"What happened?"

"Twenty-five-year-old with big tits."

"At least he's not a cliché."

Shay laughed. "He's the face you find in the dictionary under cliché. He cheated on his wife with the twenty-five-year-old intern."

"So he's a cheater." He couldn't imagine anyone cheating on the person they loved.

"He was a cheater, but he hasn't cheated on the intern wife once." She sighed. "I want to blame him. I want to say our divorce was all his fault. But I was so busy building a career, raising my brother, and taking care of Gran. There wasn't much time for him."

"That sounds like all normal things. You weren't out cheating on him. Were you?"

"No." She laughed, and it made him laugh. Her

moods were contagious. "But I wasn't home as often as I should have been. A few months ago we had some drama at home and my brother and Gran spent the night at his house. My brother now hangs at his house sometimes now. Daryn takes Gran to bingo once a month. I haven't seen him in over a year. My family is closer to my ex than I am because he spent more time with them. And when I look back, it was always that way."

Garret shrugged. "Working in law enforcement doesn't leave a lot of time for extras. Sometimes I think that was what happened with my ex. I just didn't have time for her. I was building a career." But conversation after conversation, she could never tell Garret why she wasn't happy. "She remarried a month after the ink on the divorce dried. And she's been happy ever since. At least that's what I've heard through mutual friends."

Shay nodded. If anyone could understand, she seemed like she would. "Relationships and our line of work aren't compatible."

"True." He raised his beer, she did the same, and they clinked bottles before he took a swig.

"Thank goodness for one-night stands." Shay drank.

Garret choked. When his breathing returned to normal, he picked up his fork. "We should finish our lunch." Not exactly the most baller thing to say after a woman brought up a one-night stand, but he honestly couldn't think of another thing to say.

"We should." She smiled, and with that, he couldn't seem to finish his meal fast enough.

RELATIVELY PAINLESS. Talking to Garret had been fun. Lunch had been fun. Who knew he was so much fun to talk to. They talked about family and marriages. When he talked one on one like that, he almost seemed like a good guy.

Shay hobbled to the car. A big bowl of pasta in the afternoon was not exactly the best way to keep alert.

"We still have a few hours. Did you want to go back to the hotel? Or, if you want, there's a great shooting range in Henderson. Or we could do whatever you want." Garret stumbled over the words. It would have been cute if she wasn't stumbling over her own words right now.

This was it. This was the part where she told him they should go and do a one-night stand together. Right. She couldn't even say it correctly. No one one-night stands. It wasn't even a verb.

"Are you okay?"

She hadn't even gotten in the car and she was freaking out. She hadn't even said the words. She could skip the one-night thing and they could go shoot guns or go back to the hotel. All viable options.

But that wasn't what she wanted. So, she stared at his car like it owed her money.

"Let me get you to the hotel." He opened her door and she slid inside with a thanks, waiting for him to get in the driver's side. She could do this. She could tell a man she wanted to do the nasty. Nasty, one-night-standing—she basically had the skills of a teen when it came to men.

Well, not all men. She told bad guys to fuck off on the regular. But telling a gorgeous man she wanted to do that deed left her tongue-tied like a teenager.

He made his way around the car and angled into the driver's seat. The car rumbled to life, and he backed out of the parking space. The drive down Las Vegas Boulevard was quiet. People went up and down the sidewalks, tripping from one hotel to the next. Always looking for that big meal or bigger payday, or biggest drink. They laughed and joked. They had a good time. But inside the car was silence.

She was not having a good time. They were getting closer and closer to the hotel. She didn't want to go back to the hotel. And if she didn't get her stuff together soon, she'd be spending the rest of the day playing referee between Julie and Ben—and regretting that she hadn't spoken up.

Woman up! "Why don't you show me your place?"

Silence strangled the available oxygen as her words hung in the air. With no response.

"What?" His hesitant tone said he didn't know how to respond, but maybe he really hadn't heard her. That happened when one was driving.

"I thought maybe you could show me your place. I'd love to see what the decorator did with it." There. Not throwing her body at the mercy of the court. Just wanting to see his place. Innocent.

"I'm not sure..." He stared out the windshield, and the intent look made it seem like he was warring with himself. Over what? Who knew. It was an innocent request. "Okay." He passed the customer parking and pulled into the resident lot. The breath she didn't realize was lodged in her throat spilled out. He'd said yes. Well, maybe not yes. He said okay. Not exactly the enthusiasm one looked for when propositioning a guy.

But then again, there was no proposition. It was about seeing interior decorating. Nothing more. There was no reason for her to feel slighted. "If you don't want me to come up, we can find something else to do?"

"No, it's not that." He parked his car in a numbered spot and threw a smile her way. "I want to show you."

After his car was stowed, they made their way up the elevators to the fifteenth floor. The elevator door opened to gold carpet and a hallway lined with dark mahogany doors.

At the end of the hall, Garret unlocked a door and held it open for her. The entryway was nice, and led into a true bachelor pad with a couch and chairs surrounding a large screen television. On one wall, floor to ceiling windows overlooked the Strip.

"Wow."

"I like it." He smiled. "Would you like a drink?"

"Sure." She stood at the windows, watching the buildings glimmer in the sunlight. This was it. She'd gotten this far. She just had to close her eyes and tell him what she wanted. She could do it.

CHAPTER SIXTEEN

GARRET WASN'T sure what to do—okay, he knew what to do. But he wasn't sure if he should. She seemed to want to say something, but she wasn't saying it. He really liked Shay, but the vibes were off.

He didn't play those games. He'd had a woman who couldn't tell him what she wanted once, and that had been a train wreck. He wasn't doing that again. Which sucked, because he thought Shay was different. He thought she'd fight for what she wanted—or at least be willing to talk.

He made them both a glass of water. No more beer. This was a working relationship.

"Did you want to watch TV while we wait to do the interview?" They still had to interview the dancers. Then they could go their separate ways. Although that thought was depressing. And they were here. They both had to wait. No point doing so separately.

"I do not want to watch TV." She took the glasses

from his hands and set them on a side table next to the couch.

"Um. Okay. We could go to the shooting range."

"I do not want to go to the shooting range." She ran her hand along his chest. His eyes slammed shut as every nerve ending hummed.

He wanted to tell her to stop, but he was afraid she might actually do it. "What do you want to do?" He knew what he wanted to do, but he refused to reach his hand out until she told him. He needed to hear it.

"I want to see your bedroom." Her hands traveled lower, and a groan slipped from his throat.

"Why?" His body hated him. Here he had a woman running her hands over his body, and he was asking questions. If he didn't like her so much he wouldn't care.

"If my nonverbal cues aren't enough of an indication, I want to have sex with you." She grabbed his hand and pulled him down the hall. "This way?"

He nodded. He didn't think he could form words right now. She pulled him into the bedroom, and wrapping her fingers around the collar of his shirt, she pushed him against the door.

Fucking hot.

Her mouth nibbled and sucked on his bottom lip. Her body scraped against his. Her hips. Up and down. Up and down.

He needed to taste her. It wasn't a want, it was a need. But her body moved against his and he couldn't pin her down. He had to fix that. His fingers slid through her hair and he drew her to the side, opening her up to him.

His mouth devoured. Her neck was soft and every lick sent her head further away, giving him more room to nibble and suck.

Her breaths came out in shredded gasps as his teeth scraped down her jaw and his fingertips grazed her hardened nipples through her shirt. When she groaned, his hands wrapped around the curved edges of her ass and lifted. He picked her up and pressed her against the wall. Taking control. Taking her. His mouth plunged and she took every thrust and gave it back. Her tongue rubbed his.

Her body pushed and stroked at his. His interest rose and throbbed with every swirl of her hips. She needed to slow it down, or he'd never make it to the show. He pushed on her. Trapped her as she wiggled.

His eyes found hers before she pulled off her shirt, and he slid his tongue down bare flesh, licking the edges of her bra.

"Garret," she pleaded on a short gasp. "Please take me."

She didn't have to ask twice.

He laid her onto the bed and unzipped her pants. Once they disappeared she leaned back on the bed. In bra and panties. All dark skin and pink satin. Fuck.

Every part of his body throbbed just looking at her. She was perfection. "You're beautiful."

She leaned toward him, leaving claw marks as she grabbed onto his arms. Every sting on his arm heightened the pulsing in his groin.

"I want you," she whispered as she ran her tongue along his ear.

He pulled back and ripped off his shirt and jeans in record time. Naked and harder than a quarterstaff, he yanked down the satin covering her promised land and threw them over his shoulder.

The soft mound of curls glistened for him.

"Now."

"Now what?" His finger slid along her inner thigh, just shy of those curls. He wanted to touch them—and so much more. But not till she asked.

Shay grabbed his hand and pulled him up toward her. "Fuck me, now." So demanding. Her eyes intent. She knew exactly what she wanted, and dammit if he didn't want it too.

He leaned over and dropped his lips to hers. His hips angling till he was above her. Ready to push inside. He didn't want this to be a rush job, but everything about this moment was hungry and desperate.

"Please." She wasn't begging but it was close. And if that didn't turn him on...

He found a condom in the side table and rolled it on, hands shaking, before settling in front of her. He pushed inside and held. Her body hugged his. Tight and wet. Warmth spread through him. He had to slow down or this would be about as good as a first time with a teenager.

He pulled back. Slowly feeling every massage.

"Faster." His woman begged.

And he was happy to oblige. His hips bucked and he drove into her. Her hands wrapping around his hips and moving him in and out. Fast. Hard. Body to body. He pushed to the beat she set. Shay yelled into his ear as she grabbed onto his back, nails biting into the skin.

It felt so good, so perfect as her walls contracted around him, massaging him. Bringing him to the brink. He held on, waiting for her to come first, waiting for her find that release. But every pulse of her body brought him closer and closer.

Shay bucked, her muscles clenching around him, taking him over the edge. Long stutters shattered through his body as he fell further and further over that edge. When she shuddered, her grip loosening, he leaned onto his side, keeping his weight off her. His fingers danced along her skin as she took in ragged breath after ragged breath. Her hand rubbing along his back. Both of their mouths curved in huge smiles.

After he got rid of the condom, they stayed like that in silence. Basking. Enjoying. Together. The hand at his back stopped moving. Her eyes were focused on him. "Do you need me to get you anything?"

She licked her lips and crooked a finger at him. "Just you." She looked so damn adorable, Garret couldn't help but lick his lips and join in.

WHAT HAD SHE DONE? This was supposed to be a hit it and quit it situation. Once. Not multiple times with multiple orgasms. If the sex had been crappy, mediocre even, she wouldn't want to jump back into bed with the man. But each time it had gotten better with each thrust. Which wouldn't be so bad, but she wanted to do it again. She craved it.

Dammit.

The sound of rushing water came from the bathroom. Shit. She needed to get out of there. And quick. Maybe if she hurried, she could grab a taxi and take care of the interviews alone. The way she liked it.

The sun had gone down while they were not quitting it. The room was dark. And she hadn't noticed earlier, but the drapes were closed. Honestly, she hadn't noticed a whole lot once they'd moved to the bedroom.

She slid her hand along the wall by the door. No light switch. She moved to the windows and tried to open the drapes. Nope. Why didn't anything in this place work? She moved back toward the bed and tripped over her pants. A hard surface stubbed her toe. She leaned down and pulled it out of her pocket. Yes! Her cellphone.

She turned on the flashlight option and scavenged for her clothes. Should she laugh or cry? Either way, she'd be doing it with a smile on her face.

She'd done it. She might be doing the walk of shame, hell, the scrounging for clothes of shame. But she'd done it. She'd had her fling in Vegas.

Vacation sex—check

Double orgasm—check, check.

Finding her underwear—well, that might take a little more time.

CHAPTER SEVENTEEN

GARRET OPENED the bathroom door to Shay's naked ass waving in the air. She held her cellphone like a flashlight as she crawled along the floor.

"Nice view."

She huffed and sat, leaning back against the side of the bed. "How can you tell? It's pitch black in here."

"Let there be light." He picked up the remote from the bedside table. The overhead lights turned on and the shades rose, motors whining.

"Thanks." Her eyes roamed the room, looking for something. He knew when she found it, because her eyes were glued to the ceiling and red tinged her cheeks. He looked. Her underwear hung from the ceiling fan.

She stepped onto the bed and snatched them off. "I need to get dressed."

He wrapped an arm around her as she made her way to the bathroom, arms laden with her clothes. "Are you sure? We still have some time. I've got some better ideas."

"I'm sure." She slipped through his arms and ran into the bathroom before slamming the door.

She wouldn't look him in the eye. Again. Her back ramrod straight. Again. And she ran out away from him like her ass was on fire. What the hell happened? One minute they were spooning, he goes into the bathroom for two minutes and now she's sprinting.

He slid on a pair of jeans and a button-down shirt before putting on socks and shoes. It wasn't exactly his usual suit and tie, but they were just going to do a few interviews. He didn't have the desire or the energy to get himself back in that suit.

He let Shay do her business in the bathroom without an audience while he raided the kitchen. He needed a drink. Too bad they had these damn interviews to do, otherwise he'd make his way to the bourbon. Instead, he grabbed two bottles of water. After the afternoon they'd had, she probably needed something hydrating

The water slid along the back of his throat. He grabbed the second bottle and went into the living room. There she stood, holding a picture in her hand.

"Who's this?" She turned the picture toward him. The day his mom made lieutenant. His dad beamed next to her.

"My parents."

Her brow arched. "Your mom was a cop."

"Yeah. My parents were cops until they retired last year." He looked at his mom's smile as she stood in her uniform. So proud. He handed Shay the bottle of water and grabbed the picture. "You remind me of her."

Shay nearly spit the water she'd just drank out of her mouth. "Really?"

"Really." He smiled and put the frame back on the cabinet. "She's so used to being strong for everyone, she can't stop to let anyone take care of her. It's almost like she's weak because we worry about her. But it's not like that. I don't think she's weak. I know she's strong. She can handle anything. And if I let her, she will handle everything—and everyone needs a break from that now and then."

Shay looked at him, maybe even stared. He couldn't tell if what he'd said pissed her off further, or if it might have broken through that hard shell she confined herself to. "I should go."

Pissed off it was. "I'm sorry. I didn't mean to offend."

She placed the water bottle on the glass side table. "I'm not."

"Then why are you running away from me?"

"I can't do this."

"This? What about this can't you do?"

"Nothing. I'm reading too much into it." Shay readjusted her badge and slipped on her shoes, untying and retying the laces.

"What do you think this is? Because I sure as fuck want it to be more than what just happened. Don't get me wrong, I want what just happened to happen again, preferably often, but I want to learn everything about you." He ran a hand through his hair as her focus went from him to the door. He was losing her and there wasn't a damn thing he could do about it. He held out his hand to her. He didn't know exactly what "this" was, but he was sure he wanted more of it. "Don't go."

Now he was begging, but her eyes didn't stop searching. What they were searching for, he had no idea.

"I live in Chicago."

"And I live in Vegas, but you're here now." He lifted his hand higher. "It doesn't hurt to give this a try. If it doesn't work, you go your way and I go mine."

She didn't speak. Her body was tight and stressed. She smelled like peppermint and home but she wouldn't come closer. And she was right. In a few days, she'd be on a plane to Chicago and he'd be here. Alone. Again.

But he couldn't stop himself. He wanted this time with her. He didn't care about the repercussions. And there would be repercussions. He could already feel himself falling.

What the fuck was he thinking?

SHAY WANTED to dive into Garret's arms more than anything. But a one-night stand was one night. It was in the title.

"And I live in Vegas, but you're here now." His outstretched hand begged her to take it. His eyes pleaded with her.

"When I get back, I have a new job and I'll be too

busy for anything." Not that she had anything else. With Shawn gone and her friends getting on with their work in Detectives, everyone would have their own lives to get back to. Maybe it was good she had this new job. Even if it meant being alone. A new job always meant more work. "You don't get it. Every time I get a promotion, they look at me as if I'm just fulfilling some quota. I have to prove myself again. I have to start over from scratch showing my new team I deserve this promotion. I don't have time for distractions."

Garret winced, and it killed her. He was already so much more than a distraction. She hadn't connected with someone at this level in so long.

"All I'm asking is for a chance. You may date me while you're in Vegas and realize I'm a complete idiot. This may not go past the weekend. But wouldn't you like to know?"

It sounded so logical. A few days of this sounded so good. She didn't have to overthink it. She didn't have to worry about the future. There was no future. There was just today—and hopefully tomorrow. She curved her hand into his and he pulled her to his chest. His arms wrapped around her and she melted—right into a puddle on the floor.

She could do this. Not only could she, but she wanted to do this. They might only have a few days together, but they'd make them last.

His kiss was hesitant and soft and the sizzle went all the way to her toenails. He made her feel precious, a gift. Unlike the first time, when everything was fast and demanding—this was slow and sweet.

His tongue dragged lazily along her skin. His hand skimmed under her shirt and along the hem of her pants. Her skin tingled. Her body writhed.

She'd make this last as long as she possibly could. Her body wouldn't let her stop this if she wanted to. And she didn't want to. She wanted him more than her next gasp of air.

She'd deal with the fallout later. His tongue slid along her neck and his teeth nipped at her ear.

Much later.

CHAPTER EIGHTEEN

THEY WERE A HALF HOUR LATE. *Late.* Shay didn't do late. She'd been early. She'd been on time. Late wasn't something she'd ever experienced before. But leaving the warmth of Garret's bed and his body had been so hard.

Speaking of hard—he had been. And her soft parts appreciated his hard parts. And it became so hard for her to leave him and do simple things, like put on clothes.

Garret was such a bad influence. She was making choices based on her libido and showing up late to meetings because of him. Yeah, she was blaming him. She knew it wasn't really his fault, but it was easier than admitting her own stupidity.

Heavy metal thumped through the speakers as they walked through the darkened bar area. On the stage, a dancer tore off his T-shirt. Now that was entertainment. Garret's eye-rolling and general inability to look at the stage told her he wasn't appreciating the show.

His loss.

They walked toward the bar, where Kat was bent over paperwork.

"Kat?" Shay leaned against the black lacquered bar.

Kat didn't look up. She didn't react. "You're late."

"Sorry. We ran into some difficulties." Shay tipped her head toward Garret. Not that it mattered, Kat was still staring down. "This is my associate, Garret Doyle. We're here to interview Jon. It won't take long."

"He has fifteen minutes before he has to go on." She finally lifted her head to Shay as she gathered the papers. She didn't look happy.

Not that Shay was all that happy. Did she mention how much she didn't like being late?

Shay knew when Kat noticed Garret because the scowl left her face and her tone became downright hospitable. "Follow me."

They walked through the back doors into a sea of testosterone. All of those lockers that lay dormant before now all hung open with large gorgeous men standing in front of them. Gorgeous half-naked men, to be exact.

"Jon P." Kat's voice thundered over the music.

The muscled man from last night angled his neck around the plethora of maleness. "Yeah, Kat?"

"I need you over here." Kat crooked her index finger. "These officers have a few questions for you."

"I'm getting ready. I have to be on in fifteen." Jon still had on a pair of jeans and a button-up shirt over a tank top. If his outfit from last night was any indication, he needed to lose a few layers of clothes yet.

"You can get ready while you talk, right?" Kat basically challenged Shay to say something different.

Not that Shay was going to take that challenge. She really couldn't tell him not to get ready for work. Maybe if she'd left that warm bed fifteen minutes earlier she'd have been here in time to interview him without her own personal show. Not that she was complaining.

Jon pulled off his shirt. "So, what can I help you with?"

"That's a nice tattoo." Shay tried to keep her eyes on his face but his chest muscles kept flexing and bunching.

"Thanks." Jon twisted his arm to show the full bear and sword. His looked more bear than devil. "I got it a year ago. My wife loves it."

Shay smiled. In her experience, people loved the artwork on their bodies. Any interest was usually welcome and put them at ease. "What did you do after the show last night?"

"Sorry. Need to get ready." Jon pulled down his jeans, revealing boxers. "Last night was a long night. I was up till four rubbing calamine lotion on my son's arms and legs."

"How old is your son?"

"Eight." Jon laughed. "And he loves fossils, dinosaurs, all that. We took him to Red Rock Canyon a few days ago but didn't see him roll around the poison ivy bush. The poor kid's covered in pink and high on corticosteroids."

"A prescription?"

"Yeah, his doctor gave him a small dose, but the stuff seems to knock him out." Jon slid his finger under the elastic of his boxers.

Now that would be a show.

"Maybe we could take this interview in another room—once you're dressed." Garret looked upset, maybe mad, perhaps a bit annoyed. Either way, he was cock-blocking the big reveal.

"Can they sit in your office for a few minutes while I change?" Jon asked Kat. "We can finish up in there."

"Sure."

Shay smiled as Garret followed her into the office, resting his hand on her back. Just one touch and the afternoon flooded back. Every touch. Every emotion. It had been amazing.

And she wanted to do it again. A lot. If Garret wanted to block the up-close-and-personal strip show here at the club, Shay was okay with that. As long as he didn't block what she had planned for him later.

"SO, are you buying the whole sick kid thing?" Garret let his eyes slide over the paperwork on the desk. Nothing really interesting popped out. The room wasn't big, just a cluttered desk, a tall skinny filing cabinet, and a chair. A hook on the back of the door held random clothes. It was utilitarian, if not a bit of a mess.

"Yeah, I think his kid was sick. There is too much that we could verify in the story and he's not hiding anything. The guy is an open book."

The guy *was* an open book. No matter how much Garret would love for the muscled monster to be guilty so they could move onto more fun things, this guy wasn't bad. He was a doting father and overall likable. He wasn't hedging the questions or acting like a guy who'd committed any crimes. He was letting it all hang out, in more ways than one.

"Sorry you didn't get to continue watching the show out there." Garret watched her face flush. Watching her try not to stare at the guy had been fun but watching her face flame was the highlight of his day. Okay, maybe not the highlight. After the afternoon he'd had with her, there were too many highlights to even count.

"It was a nice view, but that's okay."

"Are you sure, you seemed to enjoy it."

"Oh yeah, I enjoyed it, but it wasn't nearly as enjoyable as this afternoon."

A goofy smile took over Garret's face. He knew he looked ridiculous and dreamy-eyed, but he couldn't help it. She'd had a good time this afternoon. He'd thought she had, but hearing those words confirmed it.

He leaned over. Her lips hovering inches from his. One kiss. He felt her breath along his cheek as he pulled closer and closer...

The door flew open and—for the love of all that was holy—not only did this guy interrupt what would have been a very enjoyable kiss, but he blew into the room with a mini bandana covering his extremely generous twig and berries. And that was all. Nothing else. There was way too much skin going on in such a little room.

"Sorry about that. Do you mind if I oil up?" He held up a bottle of baby oil and began to rub it on his arms.

"Not a problem." Shay smiled. "So, you were with your son last night."

"Yeah, poor guy. Figured I'd give the wife a break. She'd been taking care of him all day." He poured the oil in his hand and rubbed it along his chest. His pecs moved up and down. Actually moved up and down on their own.

Garret reexamined the desk. Not because he was uncomfortable—much. More like he wasn't sure he'd ever be able to take off his shirt in front of a woman ever again. He looked down at his own chest, covered by a button-down shirt. Holy shit, did he feel inadequate.

Jon continued. "I have a day job and then came here, so she didn't get a chance to relax at all yesterday."

Shay sighed, a dreamy little sound. Garret could practically hear her girl parts pucker. Apparently, Jon was not only a god, he was also a saint.

Garret waited for the next question, but nothing came. There were no words. There was just the sound of oil and rubbing. He wanted to keep focusing on the desk. Vacation requests and monthly reports. All benign. He didn't want to look up at the chiseled chest and glistening skin, but the quiet was killing him.

Garret looked. Why, oh why did he look?

Jon had one foot on the manager's chair, like a mostly naked Captain Morgan, as he rubbed his legs down with oil. All of his endowments were front and center, bobbing up and down as he polished his practically hair-free body.

And Shay had given up on pretending not to look. Her stare was fixed to the guy's—assets. Her head moved up and down to the rhythm of his lubricant application.

And Jon was oblivious. He just kept oiling himself. "Is that all your questions?"

Shay's eyes drifted from his body to his face. After a second, her eyes widened and a flush fought with the normal mahogany of her cheeks.

"One more question." Garret spoke up because Shay was apparently having trouble finding her voice. It was like a porn version of an interview on *Law and Order: SVU*. Otherwise known as *Law and Order: STD*. "Do you know if anyone else has that tattoo on their right arm like that?"

Jon nodded. "Yeah, Rocket. Umm...Billy. They should be here tonight. Some of the previous dancers had it on their arm, but I don't know all of the older dancers."

"Then how can you be sure that they had the tattoo on their arm?" Shay's voice was working again.

"They have all kinds of pictures of previous dancers upstairs along the wall. You might be able to get some information there."

"Thanks." Shay shook his hand before giving him a card. "If you think of anything else, please give us a call."

"Sure." Jon took the card and headed out the door.

"So, we should probably talk to Rocket and Billy

before we take a look at those pictures," Garret suggested.

"Yeah." Shay shook her head. "This is going to be a long night."

"You're telling me." Garret stepped out the door and flagged down the manager. The sooner they interviewed these guys, the sooner they could go home together and let his fingers show how talented they could truly be and help her forget the view and the dancers.

AN HOUR LATER, they'd crossed Rocket and Billy off the list. Rocket had been bartending at his second job and Billy had left with a bridesmaid from another party. Even the pictures in the lobby hadn't given them much information.

"You ready to go back to the hotel, or did you want to grab some dinner?" Garret held open the car door as Shay angled in.

"No." She pulled out her cellphone and sent out a text before powering down the distraction. "I just told Brook I wasn't coming back to the hotel tonight."

"Did you have something in mind?"

"Oh yeah." She leaned over the center armrest. "Can you take me to your place?"

"I thought you'd never ask."

CHAPTER NINETEEN

THE NEXT MORNING, Shay walked into the unusually quiet hotel room. Quiet wasn't a bad thing. Unusual, but she'd take it. She'd spent the night wrapped in Garret's arms. They'd talked, and found other things to do with their mouths. This morning, he'd walked her to her room and they'd made out like teenagers. She was sore in places she didn't know could get sore. And tired in places she didn't know could get tired.

Maybe she'd sneak in a quick nap.

"Is the whole thing underwater?" Allison walked out of the bedroom carrying a binder, cellphone pressed to her ear. She mouthed, *you're back*, and gave a wave. "Even the pergola?" She sighed and dropped into a chair. "What should I do? I have over one hundred people coming on Saturday..."

Uh oh. Shay had heard all about the pergola at the arboretum where Adam and Allison were scheduled to exchange vows this weekend. If the place was underwater—that was not good. Finding another venue in Chicago at this late date, while Allison sat in a hotel in Vegas, would be impossible.

"And the storms aren't scheduled to stop?" Allison actually sounded like she was on the verge of tears. "All right. Call me as soon as you know something… Thanks."

Allison laid the phone on the armrest as she rested her head on the back of the chair. "Shit. Shit. Shit."

"Problem?"

"The beautiful sunny glade where my picturesque wedding was going to take place is now a swimming pool. So, unless I'm going to rent a boat and have a naval-themed wedding, we need a new venue—in six days." Allison flew from the chair and started pacing. "Six days. It took me over six months to plan this wedding, and now I need to find a location and move everything there in six days…"

Shay wanted to interrupt. She wanted to tell Allison to breathe or pause or something because Allison's face was red and her words were racing each other out of her mouth too fast for Shay to get a word in.

"…I have to call the caterer, the florist, the bakery, the guests—so many guests. How will I get in touch with them all in time? And then—"

"Don't you need a venue first?" Shay blurted.

Allison flopped into the chair and tears pooled in her eyes. "I have no venue. The wedding is off. My wedding to Adam is off."

Shay kneeled next to Allison's chair. "Breathe, Allison. Take a minute. Breathe in. Out." Shay took in a deep breath, waiting until Allison did the same. They breathed in unison until the red on Allison's face dimmed.

"Okay." Shay opened the binder and found a blank piece of paper and a pen. Handed them to Allison. "So, let's start at the beginning. Stay positive and get this done. Before we can notify anyone or do anything we need to find a new location for the wedding, right?"

"Right. In six days."

"Way to stay positive." Shay couldn't help but smile when Allison laughed.

"Okay, that wasn't very positive." Allison took in another of those deep breaths. "I can do this. New location. Most of the outdoor venues are probably having the same problem with the rain, so we need something inside. But most of the indoor venues are booked a year in advance."

"So, we need a different type of venue. Private." Shay needed to keep her focused on the task at hand and not the problems. "Do you know anyone with a yard or enough indoor space to could accommodate a wedding?"

"Adam's mother has a yard. In an emergency, we might be able to fit everyone in the house. There's not a big ballroom or anything, but we could spread out along the first floor."

"Okay good, write it down. That's a place to start."

"We have a large conference room at the Byrnes and Company building. It would be a tight fit but we could use that." Allison's voice rose in excitement.

"See. Write that down too." She hated to admit it,

but Shay was getting a little excited too. "What about your condo?"

"They have a party room. That might be able to hold everyone." Allison's pen flew over the paper before she launched her body at Shay. "Thank you so much. I was freaking out, and you knew just what to do." Allison drew back, a goofy grin on her face. "You remind me of Adam. He's like that too."

"It's a cop thing."

Allison grabbed her cell phone. "It must be. I'm going to make a few phone calls... oh yeah, I forgot. There was a guy looking for you last night. Really cute."

"Guy looking for me?" Shay was with the only guy in Vegas who would be looking for her. Her mind raced through yesterday and her little fact-finding mission at the security office. Shit. She forgot about Rick and the date she'd owed him for the file.

"Yeah, while you were on your sleepover with Garret, another guy was wondering about his date with you. Who's Rick, and why did you have a date with him?"

"Rick is no one." Shay checked to see if her nose was growing. "And I don't know about a date."

"Really?" Allison had a sad, almost disappointed look on her face.

"I was out with Garret. Why would I have plans with someone else?"

Alison sighed. "You're right. But he was so hot. I thought maybe you were double-dipping in the Vegas vacation-fling pool. You deserve to have a little fun after the nightmare you had to endure."

"Nightmare? I've been through a hell of a lot worse on the job." Shay pulled down the collar of her shirt. "This one guy stabbed me..."

Allison's face went white as a sheet, which was impressive since Allison was already pretty damn white. Maybe scaring the shit out of Adam's fiancée wasn't a good idea. Shay dragged her collar back into place and smiled. "I'm having plenty of fun, between the awards and the bachelorette party and"—*Garret*—"everything. I've had a nice time. I swear."

"Okay." Allison smiled and fiddled with her phone.

"Go plan your wedding. I'm going to change out of these clothes." The walk of shame wasn't Shay's best look—or anyone's for that matter. Anyway, she had her own call to make.

Allison took her binder and phone out to the balcony and shut the sliding door. Her phone was adhered to her ear before that binder hit the outdoor table.

Shay knew she had to make a call, but she wasn't as excited to get started. She dialed Rick and waited till he picked up.

"Hey, it's Shay."

"Shay, are you okay? I was worried about you." Rick truly sounded worried.

She was such an ass. She forgot about their date, but in her defense, she'd been extremely busy with police work and then Garret's mouth was roaming her body. Her mind wasn't really on her fake date with

Rick. "I'm fine. I'm so sorry. I was interviewing some of the guys over at the Profane from Brisbane." Most of the time anyway.

"What's going on?"

"I'm sure it's nothing." She would be able to pole vault using her nose pretty soon. "Nothing" wasn't exactly the truth, but this wasn't the time to get into it.

Silence crawled along the phone line. Rick said nothing. Maybe he didn't believe her. Maybe he did. It wasn't like it mattered. She wasn't about to start dating the man. She was a one-man woman and that man did magical things with his hands.

"I figured you were doing something important." Rick's voice lost all concern. He must have bought her deflection. "I know a few of the guys over at the Blink Hotel. I have a contact on the security team there and I could see if they've heard anything about the show. Maybe see if I can get you lists or whatever you need."

Talking to the dancers over at the Blink hadn't really produced any viable leads. They were at a standstill and running out of options. Lists. They needed an employee list.

"How about we meet for breakfast?" Rick asked.

Breakfast? That seemed wrong somehow. Wasn't breakfast a euphemism for what happened with Garret last night? And yet here she was, thinking about having actual breakfast with someone who wasn't the man she'd had euphemistic breakfast with last night. Did that make her a theoretical slut? "I don't think—"

"Come on, it's just breakfast, and I'll bring you what I can on the dancers."

Just breakfast. Seemed benign enough. And she really needed more information, or they'd be stuck at this brick wall. "Okay. I'll meet you at the buffet downstairs."

"No, not there. There's a great place called the Peppermill. It's right down Las Vegas Boulevard. I'll drive."

Alone in the car with Rick. She didn't know the guy well enough for that. "I'll meet you there."

"Really?"

"Yeah. I have an errand to run." Not really.

"Okay, I'll meet you there, then."

"Sounds great." Yep. Great. Garret was sure to understand. He knew the job came first, and it was only eggs and sausage... Maybe not the best example. It was only pancakes and syrup.

And if that pancakes and syrup led to an employee list and additional evidence, then wasn't that just a bonus?

"Let's say in n hour?"

One hour. That would give her time to shower and change. But not enough time to talk herself out of doing this. Not enough time to think about what Garret would really think. "See you then."

GARRET KEPT from rolling his eyes as Sal restarted his rampage. "She followed proper procedure, and I stand behind what LaQuitha did."

Mary snorted. "Of course, you do. You're so far

removed from what actually constitutes proper procedure—"

"Enough." Garret had been listening to these two for almost an hour. He was starting to wonder why he even bothered with their weekly touchpoint. All they did was point and all he did was want to reach out and touch them, namely slap them. "Sal, LaQuitha did the right thing handling the disturbance, but she shouldn't have thrown the guy out of the building."

"Come on, you would have done the same thing." Sal dropped his fist on the arm of the chair.

"Maybe." Garret absolutely would have wanted to do it the same, but he wasn't about to admit it. It was against the procedures. He was the manager. He had to live and die by procedures—at the very least enforce them. "But no matter what, she took things into her own hands. She should have called for assistance, and she shouldn't have thrown him out without proper cause. So, how do you want to handle it? Do you want me to?"

"No." Sal ran a hand over his bare head and sighed. "What do I have to work with?"

Mary said, "Policy states she should be on suspension without pay from one to five days." She could recite policy in her sleep.

Sal looked about ready to throttle her. "Fine, give her a one day suspension without pay." He slammed his fist again. "This is her first offense. She's a good officer."

Mary nodded. "Sounds fair."

"Good. We're all in agreement." Garret crossed

that off his list. He knew he had a smile on his face. Not even these two could take away his good mood. "Anything else?"

"The dental hygienists conference and the annual Romance Storytellers Association party are next week." Mary flipped through pages attached to a clipboard. "We're not looking at the intensity of the CMAAs, but we'll need everyone on point."

"On point for dental hygienists and storytellers?" Sal laughed. "Are we afraid there might be too much flossing and writing?"

"No." Mary glared at Sal and clutched the clipboard to her chest. "It's the numbers. We'll be at capacity, and our conference rooms will all be in play. This isn't some small get-together. This will be big. We should be prepared."

"Good point. Ask your teams if they want overtime." Garret had the best supervisors on his staff. He wouldn't get half his shit done if it wasn't for them. "I'll see you both later."

"Sure, boss." Mary walked out the door.

Sal stuck around. He always stuck around after the meeting. It gave him time to complain about Mary and whatever else was annoying him at the moment. Today Garret knew it would be all about Mary.

"So, what's with the grin?"

Or maybe not. Garret didn't want to listen to Sal pine for the affections of Mary, but he wanted to talk about the reason he had a smile on his face even less. "I'm just happy."

"Right, and who is making you so damn happy?"

Sal straightened his legs out. "Could it be a hot little Chicago cop with brown eyes?"

Garret finished writing all the notes from the meeting and slid them into a folder. "No comment."

"No comment, huh? That's new."

Garret shook his head and grabbed one of the reports from his in-basket. "Are we done here?"

Sal linked his hands behind his head and leaned back. "Mary's getting out of control."

"Mary's just fine. She agreed with your punishment."

"Yeah, that was surprising." Sal sat forward, looking genuinely confused. "I don't know why she did that."

"Maybe because it was the right call."

"Yeah." Sal stood up and headed for the door. "Nice way to deflect."

"Get to work." Garret picked up his cup of coffee. Empty. Shit. He'd never get through the pile coming in if he didn't have caffeine. He opened the bottom drawer and stuffed his hand into the K-cup box. Empty. Well, shit.

The hotel didn't supply a damn thing for the security staff, so a few years ago they'd all put money together to buy a Keurig. When they tried to pool the little pods or cups or whatever, Garret could never find the flavor he wanted. So everyone kept their own stash, except when he forgot to buy his own. Then he just took Sal's. But Sal was just as likely to do the same with Garret's stash, which was probably why the damn box was empty.

He walked out of the office. Sal and a few officers

from his team were manning the cameras. The room was mostly quiet. Mary and her people were out on the floors. Everything was running like clockwork.

Garret headed for the locker room and opened Sal's locker. A brand new box of K-cups sat on the bottom shelf. Sal must have noticed Garret was out and bought some. Was it too much to ask to share that information?

"Lost?" Rick pulled up his pants.

Garret hadn't even noticed Rick standing there. And he was half naked. The guy had an eight pack. Fuck. Garret wasn't one to get jealous, but one look at the guy's arms and abs and he could admit he was a bit jealous. And since this was the second time he'd felt that way in two days, he might need to get his ass to the gym. "Not lost. Looking for coffee." He pulled a K-cup from Sal's locker. "You heading out?"

"Yeah, I've got a date." Rick took out a T-shirt.

"Nice." A breakfast date was a little peculiar, but Garret wasn't about to judge. He was in a quasi-relationship himself and he'd take any date she'd give him, so if she wanted to eat breakfast he'd run.

He'd asked her if she'd wanted breakfast, but she'd wanted to head back to the hotel and he had to get to work.

"Yeah, I'm pretty stoked." Rick turned around and shook out his shirt. A tattoo rippled with every movement. Not any tattoo. *The* tattoo. On his forearm. Holy crap.

Why hadn't Garret noticed that before? Because he never came in the damn locker room. And he'd never seen Rick without his suit on. "Have fun."

"Planning on it." Rick put on a long-sleeved T-shirt and grabbed his wallet and keys. He practically floated out the door.

Garret tossed the K-cup back in the locker and booked it back to his office. He still had the manager's number. "Kat Drake, this is Garret Doyle. I know you won't give me an employee list, but can I ask about one of my employees?"

"Sure."

"Rick Drakos." Phone tucked between his chin and his shoulder, Garret sifted through the employee files in the cabinet. Anderson, Boggs, Cooper, Dawson—where was it? Doggett, Drakos. There.

"I don't have a Rick, but I have a Scott. He danced for us a few years ago."

"Do you know where he went?"

"After the incident, I'm not sure. He just disappeared."

"What incident?"

She snorted without humor. "The son of a bitch stole from a few of the dancers and from me. I could never prove it, but he stole my mother's watch from my purse. I was taking it to get fixed. I confronted him, and he denied it. One day, he just stopped showing up for work."

"Thanks."

"Yeah." She breathed into the phone. "I hope this Rick guy isn't related to Scott. He's a slimy son of a bitch. Take care, Garret."

Maybe it was a coincidence that this guy Scott stole jewelry from the dancers at Blink. Maybe it was a coincidence that Scott and Rick had the same last name. Maybe it was all a coincidence.

Too bad Garret didn't believe in coincidence. "Sal, get in here."

Sal stuck his head around the doorway. "What up, boss?"

"I need you to look into Scott Drakos for me."

"Is that Rick's brother?"

Garret put the phone down and grabbed his keys. "Maybe. Or it could be Rick."

"Shit." Sal ran his hand over his head. "Wouldn't we have caught it in the background check?"

"Maybe. But something isn't sitting right with this whole thing. I need to talk to Shay." Sal could work on finding the connection between Scott and Rick. Garret needed to find Shay.

CHAPTER TWENTY

SHAY INCHED CLOSER and closer to the edge of the bench seat. Rick sat next to her in the circular booth. Right fricking next to her. His long-sleeved shirt was rubbing against her skin.

She didn't want to rub and mingle with Rick. No offense to him. He was nice to look at. His shirt hugged his muscles—and they were impressive muscles. They bulged out at all the right places.

Not that Shay was noticing—well, it was hard not to notice—but she wasn't staring. Not much anyway. He was pretty, that wasn't the issue. He wasn't her type.

Now Garret—Garret was her type. He was smart and focused, and he just got her. Men generally didn't take the time to figure out what made her tick. Garret had. When he started talking about his mother and responsibility and stress, she almost reached out and jumped him. Oh wait, she did.

"Are you listening?" Her breakfast buddy frowned.

Shit. She wasn't being a good investigator. She should be focusing on getting the dancers list, not on how much and often she'd like to jump Garret. For the record, it was a lot, and often. "Yeah, sorry. I'm not very good conversation before my first cup of coffee." To make the lie believable, she took a sip of her own coffee.

"I'm the same way." He smiled and sipped his own coffee before continuing. "So anyway, LaQuitha pushed the guy out the door, and as he laid on the ground she looked him dead in the eye and, I swear, she said 'Y'all don't come back now, hear?' It was the funniest thing ever." Rick snorted. "The assholes I work for didn't think it was funny. She texted me earlier. They suspended her one day without pay. For something so stupid."

Shay couldn't exactly see the humor in the story. In fact, the only thing left unanswered was why LaQuitha only got a one-day suspension. Her words could have cranked up the drunk she'd thrown out, and then what? They could have had a fight and put others in danger. It was irresponsible.

Not that Rick could see that. One more reason they just weren't compatible. "At least it's only one day, it could have been worse."

"True. My boss is a dick. It is surprising she didn't get worse."

Garret a dick? Maybe. It was the same thought she'd had until she got to know him. Now all she wanted to think about was all the things he did to her with his di— *Bad thoughts! Refocus. Now.*

It was time to get down to business. Their food

would be here any minute, and then it would be hard to talk about anything. "So, were you able to find out any information about the dancers?"

Rick stared at his coffee mug, and a look of confusion crossed his face. At least Shay thought it was confusion. It could have been annoyance. He leaned forward and rested his hand on Shay's. No. Rested implied no movement. His fingers curled around her hand, his palm caressed hers.

It should have been nice. She liked the guy just two days ago. She thought he was hot, but something had changed.

And she knew what had changed. Garret. She wanted to share breakfast with him. Not that he hadn't offered, but he'd had to work. Not his fault.

Heck, there was no reason for this not to be nice. It wasn't tawdry or anything, but unease swirled around her gut. Her heart sped and her skin slithered. Yes, slithered. It wasn't quite bad enough to make her skin crawl, but it wasn't pleasant.

The waiter came up to the table—*thank you, waiter.* His tip just went up exponentially.

She gave Rick what was probably the most pathetic excuse for a smile in the history of smiles, before pulling her hand away. The waiter slid their breakfasts on the table and disappeared into the kitchen. Shay and Rick were alone again.

Darn waiter. Was it wrong to want him to stay? He looked like a nice enough guy. And maybe Rick wouldn't try to make hand puppets with Shay's fingers if the guy was here.

"This looks amazing, right? Best eggs in Vegas." Rick dug his fork into his plate of eggs, sausage and bacon.

"Yeah, looks good." Shay's stomach grumbled. Her own fork found its way into the pancakes and omelet on her plate.

The table was quiet as they both chewed. No hands came her way, as they appeared to be busy excavating the mound of food on his plate.

Clink. Chew. Clink. Drink.

Smile.

Clink. Drink. Clink. Chew.

For the love of all that was holy, the silence was killing her—mostly because she was still waiting for him to answer her question. The question that led to his mangling of her hands. If she didn't need the information so badly, she'd just skip it. But that list was why she was here. That list was the only reason she agreed to this meal in the first place.

"So, were you able to find any information? Maybe get that list?"

He looked up at her and gave the barest sliver of a smile. "So...don't be mad. It's too early for any of my contacts over at the show to be up. I left a message with them, but we'll see."

"Them?"

"The manager." He scooped food into his mouth with a jerky motion.

"You know Kat?"

A scowl slid right across his face, immediately replaced by a high-watt grin. She had the impression he thought she'd be knocked out by his straight white smile and sparkling eyes. Something was off.

"Yeah, we go way back."

"She's the one who said she wouldn't give us the list. If you could get that list, that would be amazing."

Rick put down his fork and slid his hand over hers. The unease returned. The slither returned. "I want to help. Let me see what I can do."

Shay tried to pull her hand back. Unease was becoming the new normal around this guy.

"I'll call her later," Rick said, still not letting go of her hand. "So, what super-secret bad guy am I helping to bust? Does this have to do with what happened to you and your friends?"

She never talked about her work. Not with anyone outside of the force—except for Garret. It wasn't anything personal. It was just the way it was. Her work and her life never mixed. No matter how much Gran begged for her to tell tales. And if Shay could turn down Gran's pleas, she sure as hell could turn down Rick. Right?

She was about to say a nicer version of that, when Rick brought her hand to his lips. "Oh, I get it." His words vibrated against her skin. "I share with you, but you don't share with me. Hardly seems fair."

No, it wasn't fair.

"Am I interrupting?" Garret loomed over the table. When the hell had he gotten there? He was pissed. His back was granite stiff and his mouth was curled in a snarl. But his eyes, they were the worst. Fire burned in that stare—fixated on Shay's hand.

The hand currently being molested by Rick's mouth.

She yanked the guilty hand into her lap, wanting to explain. But she couldn't. Not in front of Rick. He was their only lead.

"Yes, you are, Garret." Rick sighed. "Don't you have work to do?"

The same thing Garret had asked that night she'd met Rick.

"I am working." Garret turned his glare to Shay. "There's an emergency. I was sent to come and find you."

Emergency? "What happened? Is everyone okay?" Images of all the ways this could end up being a nightmare of a vacation flashed through her mind. Starting with her friends being the victim of a heist and having to spend an evening at the local hospital—oh wait, all of that happened already. What if that was suddenly the good part? What if something else happened—something worse? She didn't want to think about something worse.

She slid out of the booth and pulled a twenty out of her pocket. "I'm so sorry. I have to go."

She dropped the money on the table and started toward the door. She didn't even notice till she was nearly at the car that Garret wasn't with her.

GARRET COULDN'T BELIEVE Shay let Rick touch her. Those nasty lips on her skin. Especially after she didn't have time for breakfast with Garret.

Dammit. Garret knew he was being silly. He was the one in her bed. Unless she was just moving from one to another. He couldn't even think about that right now. He had Rick to deal with. "What are you doing here?"

"I was on a date with Shay. Nice cock-block, asshole."

Even though the words weren't used in the same sentence, Garret saw red. "You keep your cock away from Shay."

"Why? It's none of your business what I do with my cock. Or who I do it with."

"Just stay away from her." Garret leaned in, but that didn't stop this whole scene from creating a spectacle. People sat at their tables, forks hovering over food. A Metro police officer sat at the counter, looking ready to pounce.

Rick threw his napkin on his plate and slid to his feet. "Go away, old man. She doesn't want you. If you couldn't satisfy some country bumpkin who was married to you, what makes you think you can satisfy a woman like that?"

Garret's fist balled and every fucking particle in his body wanted to throw the first punch. He would throw the first and last because there was no way this guy wasn't going down. But the cop across the way was rising. And anything that Garret might do would land him in jail.

He had to be smart.

Garret leaned into Rick and smirked. "I hope you enjoyed the breakfast. It will be the last one with her."

"You can't know—"

"I know. She was barely able to keep the scowl off her face when you were molesting her hand." Garret only wished it were true. She didn't look half as disgusted as he wanted her to look.

"Fuck you, Garret."

"Come on guys. It's time to take this outside." The officer finally made his way over to the table. And the look he was throwing their way said he wasn't playing.

Neither was Garret. "I'm leaving." He couldn't finish this here. Not with the cops around and not with Shay outside. He had to get her far away from this tool and then he'd find out if that tattoo belonged to the arm that punched Shay in the face.

For Rick's sake, Garret hoped not.

But for Garret's sake, he hoped it was. He would take great pleasure in beating him to pulp.

THIS COULD NOT BE HAPPENING. If it wasn't for the cop right there, she would have gone in and separated Rick and Garret. Given how this little altercation might have to do with her, she would probably only add fuel to the fire.

Garret turned and stomped away. He walked out of the restaurant, slipping his sunglasses down over his eyes. He didn't talk, but the snarl on his lips said enough. He was pissed, and the look he gave her told her he was pissed at her.

Why was he pissed at her? She was standing here waiting for him while he played my-penis-is-bigger-than-your-penis. Waiting to find out what happened to her friends.

"What happened to my friends?" She grabbed his arm, stopping him before he reached the car.

"Nothing. Everyone is fine."

Wait. What? "You said—"

"I said that because your hands were all over Rick, and your life was in danger."

"From Rick?"

He glared and clicked the door locks open. She slid in the car. He did the same. Heavy metal blasted from the speakers when he started the car. He didn't adjust the volume. He didn't look at her.

He drove out of the parking lot and headed toward the hotel.

GARRET PULLED into his condo's parking garage and tried to control his heart rate. How he'd managed to get all the way here without the blood pulsing out of his temples, he had no idea.

His head throbbed. His body was coiled tighter than a snake. And he couldn't get the picture of that son of bitch's mouth on Shay. What was she thinking?

He leaned back against the headrest.

"So, are you going to talk to me?" Shay had the audacity to sound mad.

"Do you really want me to talk to you?" He pulled the keys from the ignition. "Because I have a lot of things I want to say to you, but not one of them is good."

"I know what it looked like, but nothing happened between Rick and me."

"What it looked like? It looked like three hours after leaving my bed you were on a date with *him*. It looked like his mouth was all over you and, dammit, you weren't pulling away." He opened the door and got out. This was getting him nowhere. Talking about it wasn't making the visions of Rick and her go away. They were just getting worse. Stronger.

He slammed the car door and leaned against the side. Breathe in, breathe out. His body was taking a bruising today and he didn't like it. He didn't want this. He'd lived through the cheating thing. He'd lived through the leaving thing. He'd lived through the broken heart. He wasn't doing that again.

A car door slammed behind him and Shay came around to face him. "I'm sorry. Rick called and told me he could get an employee list for the Profane from Brisbane. Turns out his contact there is Kat. But he thinks he can get her to turn over what we need."

"That's what I was coming by to tell you. I just got off the phone with Sal. Rick was a dancer over at Blink for about a year. Kat suspected he was stealing from the other dancers, and then he disappeared." Garret stood up. He could do this. Stay focused on the case. Forget all else. "There's no way Rick would ever get Kat to turn over anything. His name isn't even Rick, it's Scott. She was sure he stole from her, too."

Shay's face actually went ashen. Good. She was getting it.

"I saw him in the locker room today. He has the tattoo, Shay, on his arm."

"It's Rick," she whispered and stepped back. "Rick attacked us."

"Yeah. I think so. But we need proof." Garret wanted to reach out. He wanted to comfort her, but he couldn't do it. Not after what he saw.

She moved toward him, eyes wide, and Garret angled away, stepping back. Space. He needed space between them. "We should get you back to the room," he said. "We need to find Perretti, Byrnes, and Lopez. Take care of this."

"So that's it." Anger and sadness seemed to be waging war on her face.

He wanted to wipe it all away. He wanted to hold her, pretend nothing happened—pretend she hadn't ripped out his heart and stomped on it... Not helping. Focus. "We have some work to do, but we'll find the proof we need."

She turned from him and headed toward the hotel side. "Fine."

"Wait." He reached out and grabbed her arm. It was instinct really—a really bad instinct.

"For what?" She yanked her arm away.

This was so much easier—this anger. He couldn't deal with upset Shay. Pissed Shay was better. He just had to keep her talking. "Don't you want to figure out a plan?"

"A plan?"

"How we're going to proceed."

"Well, you seemed all gung ho on telling Perretti, Byrnes, and Lopez a minute ago. You were practically running away."

Yeah, he had been. And he had tried to run away. Why wasn't he doing that now? Why wasn't he trying to run away from her?

The visions of Shay and Rick hadn't subsided. His anger hadn't gone away. But the thought of losing her. Fuck. The thought of her going back to Chicago without being in his arms just one more time physically hurt. He couldn't stay mad.

Shay sighed. "Don't you want to include the local PD?"

What did they have to do with Shay and Rick? Oh yeah, they were having a conversation that had nothing to do with Rick's mouth all over her body... Would she have let it get further if he hadn't stopped them? Would he have followed her to Chicago? Fucking Chicago.

He had bigger problems than Chicago. Metro. He couldn't get them involved. Not with what he was planning. "We don't need Metro, yet. We can handle it." He knew he was lying as the words left his mouth. Not about needing Metro, more that the cops would expect to be informed of any progress. But no matter how much he wanted to include them, something was stopping him. Not something. Rick. He wanted to bring the guy in. He wanted to take the jackass down. He wanted him to suffer, and if Rick suffered at Garret's hands that would be a bonus.

"Are you sure? If we were in Chicago, I'd want to be in the loop—"

"We're not in Chicago."

"I get that." She sighed. "Let's go back to my room. We'll get the guys and come up with a plan."

"I have things to do in the office first." Lying was easier and easier. "Go find the guys and we'll meet up."

"Are you sure?"

"Yep. Go ahead." He watched her walk toward the hotel. He didn't need Metro getting in the way of this takedown. And he sure as shit didn't need the Chicago Police Department with their nose in it, either.

Rick was his employee. His shitty, lazy employee, somebody Garret should have gotten rid of long ago. Now was his chance. He needed to check Rick's residence. Find something, anything to tie him to the attack and then Garret was going to deliver Rick's ass to Sergeant Dickinson over at Metro. If Rick wanted to be combative as Garret brought him in—

Icing on the cake, right?

CHAPTER TWENTY-ONE

SHAY SAT on the couch while Byrnes paced the floor. Perretti leaned his head back, and Lopez played some game on his phone.

"Where the hell is he?" Perretti asked the ceiling for the third time. No one knew the answer twenty minutes ago, so Shay guessed no one knew now either. Especially the ceiling.

"He said he had to do something in the office and then he'd be up." Shay figured it would take a few minutes, but it had been over a half hour since she'd left Garret in the garage.

"Screw this." Lopez shoved his phone in his pocket. "Let's just go to his office and pull him away from whatever shit he's got going on. We can't just sit here. We're giving this Rick asshole time to get away."

Shay hated to admit it, but Lopez was right. They needed to move.

Somebody knocked on the door, and Byrnes

jumped up to answer it. "About time." He whipped it open. "Where the hell have you been?"

Silence. Then Byrnes stepped back, revealing a shocked-looking Sal. Probably because Byrnes screamed in his face.

Shay stood up. "I'm sorry. We thought you were Garret."

"What do you mean? I thought Garret was up here with you." Sal frowned.

Last she checked, Garret was a grown man. Just because he wasn't exactly where Sal thought he was supposed to be wasn't a reason to be worried. Was it? "He said he had some things to do in the office, and then he'd come up and meet us."

"I just came from the office—his office. He's not there. He hasn't been there since after the team meeting this morning."

A stab of worry poked at Shay. "Then where is he? We were supposed to head over to Rick's. Would he have gone alone?"

"Shit. I hope not." Sal ran a hand over his balding head. "We found some information on this guy. His real name is Scott Drakos. He's got a rap sheet longer than Santa's naughty list. It's not just petty shit either." Sal handed Shay a folder. "Aggravated assault and battery, attempted murder... The list goes on."

Shay clenched the folder in numb fingers. "How is he working for you? How did he pass the background check?"

Sal shook his head. "He used his brother's name. We've contacted the company that runs our background checks to find out how he faked his fingerprints and everything else. Turns out that they had let go of an employee who was taking bribes. Since Rick Drakos claimed he didn't have a concealed carry permit, they didn't check any further. Rick is actually some computer engineer in New York."

"Doesn't all of your security team carry?"

"No. Only a handful of us have a concealed carry permit." Sal shook his head. "The casino doesn't allow guns, period, anyway."

"Makes sense." Shay's eyes skimmed over the pages. Sal wasn't exaggerating. This guy was some kind of messed up. And Garret might be heading right to him. Rick or Scott didn't seem like the type of guy who would go quietly. Shit. "Does Garret know this?"

"No. I've been trying to call him, but he's not answering. I checked his condo and then came here."

That stab of worry was now a gash of oozing concern. "We need to get to Scott's." Shay reached for her gun—that she didn't have, and her knife, which was in Chicago. Son of a...

"We need to think about—" Perretti rested his hand on Shay's arm.

"Think about what? We don't have time to sit here and play games. We need to hit the road. We'll figure out a plan on the way." Shay snatched the keys for Byrne's rental car off the table. The damn thing would have come in handy over the past few days, but she'd been confined to using Uber and taxis. "I'm driving." She twirled the key on her finger.

Large hands swooped in and stole the fob. "My rental. I'm driving."

"Fine. Drive. But let's go," Shay said as she walked out the door. If Byrnes knew what was good for him, his ass and his keys were following her down the hall.

She hit the down button on the elevator and looked back to see them all walking up behind her.

"How should we play this?" Sal drew his gun and checked the clip. "We can't exactly go in guns blazing. We only have one gun, I'm assuming."

Everyone shook their head. With guns banned during the awards show, when they would've needed them, what was the point of bringing their guns on vacation to Vegas?

"Aren't you like, dating this guy?" Lopez leaned against the wall.

"What does her dating Garret have to do with anything?" The elevator doors swung open and Sal held the door for Shay.

"Garret? She went on a date with Scott this morning." Lopez followed her into the elevator. "Why don't you just call him up? See what old lover boy is up to?"

Sal's face went from confusion to disgust and then realization. "That's why he went after him."

"Probably." Shay shook her head to remove the guilt. It wasn't working. The guilt was still punching a hole in her chest. "But it wasn't like that. I wasn't dating Scott. I went to breakfast with Scott to find out what he knew. It was a fact-finding meal. Not a date."

"Does Scott think it was a date?" Sal hit the button and the doors shut.

Had he thought it was a date? If he had, didn't that make her a shit for leading him on? "Yeah." Yeah, he thought it was a date and yeah, she was a shit. She should've handled things differently, but she hadn't known. And anyway, Scott was a slimeball who stole other peoples' stuff and beat the crap out of women. So what if she led him on?

None of that fixed the guilt. Garret had been devastated.

"Calling him might not be a bad idea," Lopez said as the elevator door flew open.

"But he saw Garret and I together," Shay pointed out.

They piled out of the elevated and hurried through the casino to the door leading to the parking garage. The stifling Vegas heat hit her right in the face. The air of the garage wasn't cool-shade like back home. The heat was dry.

"True, but if he's not home, we might be able to catch him before Garret does. Bring him in without a fight." Byrnes sounded like the voice of reason, but Shay hated this reasoning. She didn't want to make things worse with Garret. She didn't want to call Scott.

"Shay." Perretti threw himself into the back seat of the rental car. "It's our best option."

"Fine." She pulled out her cell phone and flipped through the contacts as four guys stared. They waited and listened. There was no way in hell she was having this conversation in front of them. "Give me a minute. Alone."

She heard a ring back tone before Scott picked up.

"Shay, is everything okay? You ran out of breakfast like your ass was on fire."

"Yeah. I wanted to apologize. Are you home?"

"Yep. Just watching some TV." His tone turned from serious to playful. "Want to come join me?"

"Actually, yeah. I was hoping to stop by."

"I'll text you my address. I can't wait to see you."

"Great." She disconnected the call and slid into the front seat of the car. Sal and Lopez sat in an idling SUV behind them. At least she didn't have to listen to Lopez or see the judgment written on Sal's face. She deserved it, but that didn't mean she wanted to hear it. She thought about that call as Byrnes drove down the ramps and into the sun. She'd actually heard the smile in his voice.

Garret would hate her going anywhere near that man. Garret would hate that tone. She was such a shit.

"SHAY'S COMING TO SEE ME." Scott leaned against the couch and smiled. "That's got to piss you off, huh?"

No response.

Scott propped his feet on the table. The house needed a little cleaning before Shay got here, but nothing he couldn't do in a few minutes. Most of his shit, except for the jewels and money, was shoved in the back of his car, parked behind his townhouse. They'd wanted five hundred extra a month to use one of the garages. Hell no. He would never pay that kind of scratch for something so stupid. So what if it meant he had to walk a block to get his car? It was good exercise.

In a few hours, it wouldn't even matter. He'd be on the road and Las Vegas would be a distant memory.

But first things first. He was spending time with Shay. So he needed to get ready.

He got off the couch and picked up his new toy—Garret's gun—from the table and stuffed it in the waistband of his jeans. He'd relieved the asshole of his gun before he started shooting up the place. Garret never did have any respect for other people. So why would have respect for Scott's home?

Scott huffed and crossed the room. "She likes me. She likes me more than she ever liked you. But that's not unusual. Why would any woman want someone like you, when they could have someone like me?"

Thump. Scott's shoe slammed against Garret's cheek.

"She knows I'm a better man than you."

Thump. Thump.

"Can't argue, can you?" Scott kicked at Garret's head again, so his head thumped against the floor. Garret was such a pansy. He'd stopped responding a few minutes ago. Couldn't take a little beat down. "What an asshole."

His boss treated him like shit all the time. For no reason. Well, Scott knew the reason. Scott was better looking, more successful, and just better. Garret was jealous. Shay probably wouldn't understand why he'd had to knock Garret on his ass. And he didn't have time to explain.

He dragged Garret by the arms into the spare bedroom. After he locked the door, he checked the hallway. It was a mess. Broken molding where Garret fell. Cracked wallboard where Scott fell. Not that Scott had passed out like a pansy. There was actually too much work to do to make this shithole presentable. Too much work for a little piece of tail.

He should just grab the money and go. He could find someone in his new place. He wasn't really sure where he was heading. Maybe the mountains of Montana, or maybe a big city—Houston, Miami.

Fuck it. He was done playing games. Shay was hot, and he would love to tap it, but he wasn't taking a chance on getting caught. It wasn't worth it. She wasn't worth it. She'd probably called from the hotel. He had at least ten more minutes before she got here.

He needed five.

In the master bedroom, Scott stood on the corner of the king-size bed and reached over his head. He unlatched the grate for the air duct and let it swing down. Sliding his arm inside the duct, he dragged a canvas bag out and dropped it on the bed. One more.

His fingers found the handle of the other canvas bag. This one was heavier. When he yanked at it, dust and random crap landed in his eyes. He hated leaving his shit in the ceiling. There was probably asbestos and other deadly crap falling onto his face.

God, how he wanted a shower now. But he didn't have time. Not with Garret locked in the next room. Too many variables. Hopping off the bed, he slid the blinds to the side. No unusual cars on the street, or cops approaching the door. He had time. He double-checked the contents of the bags. A few pieces of jewelry. A few thousand dollars. Enough to pay his rent and car payment. Things he wouldn't have to worry about if he was in the wind. He looped the bags over his shoulder.

The doorbell chimed. Shit. He thought he had more time.

Scott gave his bedroom one last look, making sure he wasn't leaving anything behind.

It was really a shame. This town wasn't that bad. Sports books on every corner and willing women in every bar. Although it was probably for the best. Things were getting a bit too dicey around here. He needed a change of pace. A fresh start.

The bell chimed again. Just give up. He jogged to the back door and peered out the window. No one was there. Yet. He opened the door just as he heard voices around the side of the building. He shut the door and headed for his car.

Good luck finding him in...Houston? He'd always wanted to try Texas.

CHAPTER TWENTY-TWO

SHAY GLANCED up and down the block as she waited for Rick to answer the door. Cracked sidewalks and dirt lawns everywhere the eye could see. She knew he was here. She'd seen the blinds move when they'd pulled up.

"I checked Garret's car. He's not in there." Sal came up next to her and peered between the opening in the blinds. "Looks like no one's home."

"We just saw him." Shay hit the doorbell again.

Nothing. Other than the chime, no sound. This was ridiculous. Garret and Scott had to be in there.

"Rick." She pounded on the door, glad she remembered to call him Rick and not Scott. Having a bad guy with two names was annoying. She knocked again. Nothing.

"Screw this." Lopez vaulted over the crispy bushes lining the walkway to the house. "Let's go in through the back. Shay and Sal, take the front. Joe, watch the windows."

"Who put you in charge?" Byrnes followed his partner around the side before Lopez could reply. Maybe he replied. Shay didn't care. She wasn't in the mood for their antics. Maybe after they found Garret—safe and sound—she'd be interested in anything anyone had to say.

Now? Not so much.

"Let's go." She tried the doorknob and it opened. That was easy.

The living room looked uneventful. Nothing out of the ordinary. White walls. A light brown couch, matching chair, and a big-screen TV. No lamp or pictures on the black plastic side tables. It barely looked lived in. Sal checked the front closet. Empty.

Completely empty.

"Does this guy even live here?" Sal whispered, and headed down a hallway littered in debris. Something happened here. Shay followed Sal as Lopez and Byrnes came right through the kitchen. Nothing was locked.

Shay approached the first door in the hallway and twisted the knob. Locked. Having the door unlocked would have been way too easy.

"We'll hit the next one," Byrnes whispered as he and Lopez slid behind Shay and Sal. He turned the knob and voila, the door opened.

Shit. Shay stared at the locked door. This wasn't good. You only locked doors when you didn't want someone to get to something. What if Scott was torturing him in there?

The look on Sal's face told Shay he was thinking something similar. "Stay back." Sal pushed her to the side. He leaned against the opposite wall and aimed a kick at the knob, busting the door wide open.

The room was empty. Almost. In the middle of the empty room lay a body. Not just any body. Shay knew that body. She knew the planes of his abs— his lips—his hands as they roamed all over her.

Garret. Lifeless. Not moving. A sob pressed against her throat. *Oh no. Oh no. Oh no.* She dropped to her knees next to him. *Please say something, Garret. Anything.* Hell, she'd even take April Fools right about now. She grabbed his hand, careful not to move him. She knew the rules.

"Garret." The word somehow scraped past her lips. She searched his neck with her fingertips and found a low pulse. "Call an ambulance. He has a pulse."

Sal dialed before handing his phone to Shay. "Take this. Guys, we're in here."

She clutched the phone and nodded. Maybe. She might have nodded. Someone came on the line, but all she could think about is how close she was to losing Garret. Was he even hers to lose?

Shay curled her hand around his and held on for dear life. She shouldn't be this attached. This shouldn't upset her so much. He was a coworker. Not even a coworker. Someone she just met. But watching his chest rise and fall in short bursts was killing her.

What if he didn't wake up? What if this was good-bye? The last thing he'd done was move away when she'd leaned into him. He wasn't even hers. Yet here she sat, heartbroken.

Garret's eyes flew open.

"Garret!" His name ripped from her throat.

FUCK. *Fuck. Fuck.*

Scott hit the steering wheel and breathed out through clenched teeth. He forgot his fucking keys. He hadn't locked it, which was a plus, but without the keys he wasn't going anywhere.

Every day, he left for work or the gym and remembered his keys. But today, the day when he truly needed them, he left them on the counter. No way in hell he was going back into the townhouse. Not with Shay and her little minions running around his place.

They'd probably found Garret by now. A siren, in the distance but getting closer, confirmed that suspicion.

If he couldn't get his keys, what the hell could he do? Hotwire the car? Of all the shit he'd done over the years, he'd never actually stolen a car. Well, not without the keys. He took Valerie's car after he'd found out she cheated on him, but he'd had keys to that crap bucket.

Messing with wires and electricity seemed like a really dumb idea. And when his friend from juvie had told him about getting zapped from twisting the wires, Scott knew that would never be something he'd need to learn.

But now. He needed to learn. Quick. And where do you learn to do random shit? Google.

He pulled out his cellphone and Googled "How to hotwire a car". Holy crap, there was a lot of information on the subject. *How to hotwire a car in seven simple steps.*

Seven steps. How easy was that?

Got to love the internet.

Step 1: Only hotwire a car that belongs to you.

Really? Like that would stop anyone from using this information to steal a car. "Oh, I can't take this car, the internet told me not to." Stupid.

Step 2: You must be able to get inside the car.

He was in the car. So far, he was two for two. He was flying through these steps. Hopefully they'd all stay as easy as the first two had been. If so, he might look into stealing cars as a new hobby.

Step 3: Remove plastic cover on the steering column and find wire connectors.

Plastic cover. Plastic cover. He ran his hand along the steering column. There was a swivel so the wheel could be raised and lowered. There was a steering column. But there was no fucking cover.

He tried pulling on the dashboard. Maybe he could get to the connector thing through there. Didn't budge.

Crap. He looked back at the Googler in his hands. Maybe he went to the wrong instructions. He scanned the tiny screen.

Only cars built before the mid-nineties are good candidates for hotwiring. Any car built after those dates has built-in security to prevent hot-wiring.

Well, fuck. That meant his 2007 Mustang wasn't going anywhere. Which meant he needed another way to get out of town. Someone had to have a car he could take off their hands.

CHAPTER TWENTY-THREE

HIS HEAD POUNDED, and all Garret saw were faces staring down at him. Lots of faces. He recognized them all, but why did they look so concerned? Where the hell was he?

"Shay, honey, why are you crying?"

The look of horror on Shay's face made him wonder if he was on his deathbed. Or if she didn't like being called honey.

Little bits came back. He was at Rick's. Or Scott's. He'd come to haul his thieving ass to jail. Garret couldn't see Scott's face. All he saw were cops, and Garret was flat on the floor. Shit. Scott must have gotten away.

Garret pushed until he was sitting, legs out in front of him. His head swirled in a tilted whirl of greens, blues and reds. He closed his eyes until the colors faded. He could do this. He was okay.

He bent his legs, preparing to stand.

"No. Sit. You were hurt." Shay rested a hand on his

shoulder. It might not have been Shay's. The hand was huge, but the voice was hers.

"I have to get Scott." He made it to his feet with minimal spinning rainbows.

"The ambulance is coming." Shay looked so concerned. For him. She was worried about him.

Memories of the conversation he'd had with Scott flooded back. Scott was planning on sleeping with her. The thought brought bile up the back of his throat. "What happened?"

"When we got here, he was gone, and you were locked in this room." Shay's tears had disappeared, but her eyebrows were scrunched in concern.

He couldn't help the smile. She was concerned. That meant she cared about him. She wasn't worried about Scott...

Fuuuuuuck.

"He has my gun."

Shay's brows drew lower, if that was even possible. "Your gun? When did you grab a gun?"

"I have one in a trunk safe for emergencies." Garret headed toward the door but was stopped by a big hand on his shoulder. Definitely not Shay.

"Let us handle it, boss." Sal's grip was firm. Resolute.

Boom!

A gunshot pierced the air. *Scott.*

"Go get him," Garret called to the men standing around him. When Shay tried to follow, he took her hand. "Stay here with me. He has a gun."

"I face them every day." She was going. He knew she was going after her partner and her coworkers.

He placed his lips on hers. She was hot and real and he hated fighting with her. "Be careful."

Her lips found his again. Soft and gentle. The kind of kiss that said she wanted him. The kind of kiss that said she cared about him. The kind of kiss he wanted more of...except his gun was in someone else's hands.

He pulled away. "Go." She smiled and ran out the door.

Garret was right behind her. There was no way he'd let them go out there alone. His gun, his responsibility. If someone needed to jump in front of Scott as a diversion, a target, he'd do it. There was no way he'd let Scott hurt any one of his friends. No way.

No matter what the cost.

SHAY RAN out of the townhouse just in time to see Scott drag a woman from her car and throw her into the street. The woman clawed and argued and made an overall fuss, but he had a gun. Which should have told the woman to hand over the car and walk away. This woman hadn't gotten the memo.

People were stopping. Staring. Dammit. The more civilians, the more chances for things to go wrong. And this had all the makings of something that could go wrong.

The woman threw the keys to her son and told him to run. The kid took off. Too fast for Scott. The woman scrambled to her feet as Shay ran closer. Scott's rap sheet hadn't said anything about killing, but he could up his game at any time.

He grabbed the woman's arm. Aimed the gun at the woman's head.

"Scott. Stop!" Shay was a few feet away, hands in the air. She didn't want him to get the idea that she was armed. Because she wasn't.

Scott's eyes were wide as he watched Shay approach. Maybe because he realized she used his real name. Shit.

He dragged the woman to her feet, pulling her close to him. The gun was firmly lodged against her temple. "Everyone stay back, or I kill her." He tightened his grip as she squirmed. "I need a car."

"Please don't take my car. I need it to get to work." The fact that a crazy person had a gun to her head didn't seem to faze her.

"If you don't stop squirming, you won't have to worry about work anymore." Scott ground the barrel deeper into her temple.

She whimpered.

"Let her go." Sal stood off to the side. His gun raised.

Scott pulled the woman up higher against his chest. "Give me your keys."

Shay put her hand on Sal's before he could do anything. "Adam, give him your keys."

Adam gave Shay a look but pulled out the key fob and tossed it over. Scott caught the fob and hit the button. A car beeped from the front of the house.

"What is it?"

Adam glared at Scott and didn't seem to want to answer the question.

"Fuck it. I'll just see which car's lights flash. Scott inched around the side of the townhouse toward the front yard, woman-shield in place. They moved quickly, Scott pulling her and watching the cops at the back. He made around the building and pushed the button on the fob. Adam's rental beeped and the lights blinked.

Scott pushed the hostage in the driver's door and over the center console to the other side of the car. His gun stayed on her. His eyes stayed on everyone who had followed him to the car.

He started the car and pulled away from the curb.

Shay watched Scott drive down the street and take a right. "We need to follow them. Now."

"I'm driving." Sal went around to the driver's side.

"I'm going with you." Shay threw open the passenger door while Lopez and Byrnes opened the back doors. "You'll need backup."

"Perretti, stay here and wait for the cops."

He mimicked a salute and went off to lock down the scene.

"Thanks for suggesting they take the rental. I'm liable for whatever shit he does." Byrnes's pout was evident in his tone.

"Didn't you get the insurance?" Shay did up her seatbelt as Sal shot off like a rocket down the road, taking the first right. Scott's car was in front of them—way, way in front of them, but they could catch up. As long as Sal did some creative driving. Sirens wailed behind them as the local cops probably pulled up to the scene.

"I got the insurance." Byrnes nodded, but still looked like a kid who'd been grounded from video games.

"If we lose him, the rental company has trackers in the car." She saw when realization hit all three of the men. She nodded to Sal. "But let's not lose him."

Sal smiled and hit the gas. He passed a few cars. Shay knew he was trying to get around the cars without hurting anyone—without causing any accidents. She appreciated it. But she also wanted to get closer to the jerk before he somehow disappeared.

"He took a left at that big palm tree." Shay pointed where Scott had just turned—a good half a mile up. Shit. Her knee bounced while she watched the intersection, wondering if he was still on the road he'd just turned down. He could have taken another left, a right, or found a place to hide.

Another car took that left. Black SUV. She'd swear that was Garret's car. That couldn't be right. It couldn't be his car. They'd left him back at the house waiting for the paramedics. Right?

"Did you see Garret's car when we left?" She said the words out loud, hoping someone had noticed.

A round robin of noes and I-wasn't-looking came from the car. She picked up her cell and dialed. Although she wasn't sure why she even bothered. The pit in her stomach told her she knew the answer to the question. "Perretti, have the EMTs taken a look at Garret yet?"

"Ummm...no. He's not here. I figured he was with you."

"Is his car out front?"

"Hold on." A shuffling noise came through the phone and then he was back. "No black SUV out front." A deep voice screamed something muffled over the line. "Look, I have to go. We're in some shit here. The Las Vegas cops aren't all that appreciative of our work on this case. They're threatening to call our chief. They've already sent some uniforms after you and Scott."

"Shit. Try to stall them. Maybe if we deliver Scott to them, they'll be more forgiving."

"Just get the son of a bitch. Quick," Perretti whispered before hanging up.

Sal finally made the left. Shay's eyes scanned the road. The rental was gone, and Garret's car was nowhere in sight.

They lost him. Shit. What the hell were they going to do now?

CHAPTER TWENTY-FOUR

GARRET PRESSED a hand to his side and winced. That son of a bitch must have broken one of his ribs. He vaguely remembered the lucky shot that asshole got in, knocking Garret's head against the doorframe.

Speaking of... Garret probed the knot on the side of his head. That son of a bitch was going to pay for getting the jump on him. Okay, that wasn't even the worst thing Scott had done. The way he talked about Shay—the things he'd said—Garret wanted to rip off his head. And if Garret was lucky, he'd still get that chance.

Garret kept his distance as Scott merged onto I-15. He was either heading to Los Angeles or San Diego. Shit. Or not. Mexico. If the guy was smart, he'd be heading out of the US altogether. And despite the fact that he'd done some boneheaded shit when he'd worked at Pura Vida, Scott seemed to be smarter than he appeared.

The woman still sat in the passenger seat, and she

appeared to be alive. Her head tilted back and forth and her mouth seemed to be moving every time Garret got a glimpse of her. She must be driving Rick nuts. If she wasn't in such danger, the thought would make Garret pretty fucking happy.

Laughing at Scott's discomfort wasn't something Garret had time for. He needed to find a way to stop Scott from getting out of Vegas. Metro was already involved, but once Scott left the county, they'd get other departments to help. Nye county. Highway patrol. California. The cops would be ten deep if they didn't stop Scott. It would be a cluster Garret didn't want to deal with.

The cellphone in his pocket chirped. Again.

Sal's phone number popped up on the dashboard screen. Sal's truck had been behind him for a few miles, but Scott had lost them. Garret was the only one on Scott's tail.

Garret hit the button on his steering wheel and answered the call.

"What the hell are you doing?" Shay didn't sound all that happy.

"Hello to you too." He switched lanes and slowed down to keep his distance. Scott hadn't realized he was being followed. Garret wanted to keep it that way.

"You're supposed to be getting checked out by the EMTs. You're not. Where are you?"

"Driving. I'm thinking toward California."

"I-15?" Sal's voice came over the line. They must be on the car speaker.

"Yeah."

"We're a few minutes away." Sal's voice was muffled, as if he was turning the car around. "We'll come to you."

"We need to stop him." Shay's voice cut in, sirens in the background. Reinforcements must be tailing them.

"I'm open to suggestions." And he was. He'd take anything at this point that didn't include crashing his car into Scott or shooting out tires on a busy interstate.

"Does he know you're following him?"

"No. So keep your distance. He knows what your car looks like, right, Sal?"

"Yeah. Got it." Sal's car blinker tapped in the background during a silence. The sirens stopped howling. They were all aiming for the element of surprise. Words hung in the air. Garret could feel something swirling across the line. They had something to say.

"Are you sure you should be driving?" Shay broke the silence.

Ah. Now he got it. They didn't think he should be out after his beatdown. Scott shouldn't have gotten any strikes in, let alone enough to knock Garret on his ass. He was better than that. But Garret had gone in cocky, he'd been distracted, and he'd let that asshole get the upper hand.

Yeah, his ribs hurt and there was a gash above his eye that seemed to have its own pulse, but really, his ego had been hurt the hardest. He wasn't going to lay down and let this guy get away. He needed to fix his mistake.

Scott's car swerved into the far-right lane, and he

took the off-ramp to I-160. Garret followed. A few beeps, and probably some cursing, was left in his wake.

"What's going on?" the spectators on the cell phone called out. He'd almost forgotten about them.

"I think Scott made me. He turned off onto 160." Garret drove along the ramp, keeping his eyes on the rental a few hundred yards up. Scott took a side road. He thought he'd lose Garret. Garret hit the gas. Not today. Scott wasn't getting away that easy.

"Toward Pahrump?"

"Yeah." The miles flew past as they sped down the highway, away from the city and toward the looming Spring Mountains. The cars were fewer and farther between on the two lanes of traffic. But once they hit Pahrump there would be more people, more ways this could go south.

Garret had to end this now. He pulled alongside the rental car. With a silent prayer of regret to the car gods, he eased the wheel of his very new, very nice SUV to the right until he bumped Scott's car. Then he turned harder and hit the gas.

Scott's car spun away from Garret, the front wheels leaving the road and hitting the dunes on the side of the road. Up. And. Down. Up and down. Brake lights flashed red through the sand-filled air.

The rental car slammed into a dune. The airbags deployed.

Silence settled over the car. No roar of the engine. Garret pulled over, put his SUV in park and stepped out.

Scott's door flew open and the gun glinted in his

hand. The woman was yanked across from the passenger side and through the open door. "Come on. We're going for a walk."

"Where are we going to walk? We're in the middle of nowhere." The woman stumbled after him.

"Let me worry about that."

Scott didn't need to worry about that because there was no way Garret was letting them go anywhere. "Scott, I'm just here to talk."

"Bullshit," Scott yelled, turning to face Garret while walking backward. "You never talk. You lecture. You bitch. You boss. You never talk."

"Now I have motivation. I want to listen. What are you going to do—walk to Pahrump?" Just keep him talking. That's all Garret needed to do until help arrived.

"None of your business."

"Turn yourself in. Come on and think about it. You'll never make it out of the desert alive."

"Shut up, Garret. Why are you always such an asshole?"

"Fine. I'm an asshole. Use your brain. People die out here." Garret shook his head. "If you're going to commit suicide, at least leave her here with me. She can't handle the walking or the dehydration."

"Give me your car keys." Scott moved toward Garret.

"What?"

"We're getting out of here." Scott shook the gun at Garret. "Give me your keys, or I shoot the girl."

"You're not a killer. Don't do this."

"I'm not asking again." Scott pulled the trigger, and the shot sent up a plume of sand in front of Garret.

"All right. All right. Just calm down." Garret tossed the keys at Scott's feet.

Scott shoved the woman forward but didn't let her go. "Pick them up."

She leaned over and grabbed the keyring, and Scott jerked her upright. "Just stay where you are," he told Garret.

Garret didn't move. It took everything in him not to jump the man. But even if Scott's aim was awful, he might get out a lucky shot. Right now, he was all that stood between that woman and freedom. He couldn't make a mistake.

Scott inched back over rock and sand, keeping Garret in his sight.

A voice from over by the road yelled, "Scott Drakos, drop your gun!" Garret didn't dare react to the sound of Shay's voice.

"Get back, Shay," Scott yelled back. The gun wavered, from Garret to Shay and back.

"Look, I'm not coming any closer," Shay called out. "Just leave the woman here with us. You go. You don't need her weighing you down."

"Yeah, right. I'm sure you'll let me go on my merry way after I hand her over. Do I look stupid?" He slid sideways, his back to the SUV.

Five feet. That was all Scott needed to reach the SUV and get away. Garret couldn't let that happen. He had to wait for him to make a mistake. And he would.

Scott inched back. One foot. Two feet. The

woman's ankle snagged on a branch and she stumbled. He tried to keep her on her feet, but she flopped into a puddle onto the ground.

Garret saw the moment Scott made his choice. He left the woman where she was and ran the last few feet to the car. He wrenched open the driver's side door and jumped in.

Garret ran toward Scott as the engine sparked to life. He was getting away.

At the same time, Sal slid out from behind the car and whipped open the driver's side door. He pressed his gun against Scott's temple. "Hands above your head."

"I thought you said if I let her go, you'd let me go."

"I never said that," Sal said, and Garret had to smile. A win for the good guys.

CHAPTER TWENTY-FIVE

SHAY COULDN'T GET THERE FAST ENOUGH. One second Sal was sliding behind the car while Scott yelled at Shay. Then Sal had the door open and was telling Scott to put his hands above his head. The next second a loud bang filled the air and Sal dropped like a stone.

It happened that fast. It happened on her watch.

"Get the gun." Adam ran toward the hostage. "I'll get her out of the way."

The door to the SUV slammed, and the tires screeched as Scott pulled onto the road, dust kicking into the air.

Shay scooped up the gun, barely registering the sight of Garret applying pressure to Sal's wound. She aimed at the SUV. Dammit. Bad angle. She ran two steps. She wasn't letting this asshole get away. She aimed for the back tire. Fired. Nothing. She hit the other tire, and luck was with them because the SUV spun, hitting the ditch at the side of the road.

The burst of the airbag deploying came from the car and then nothing. No one came out. The door didn't open. Nothing.

Shay jogged to the side of the car and watched. Scott's head didn't move. She made her way to the driver's side door and whipped it open.

Scott's head lolled to the side—his eyes closed. His hand...

The gun. Garret's gun was on Scott's left thigh. His hand wrapped around the grip. Shit. She needed that gun. But was Scott really out, or was this some sort of game? She kept her own gun on him.

Movement at her side. Garret. "Take this." She gave Garret her gun. The last thing she needed was for Scott to get that away from her. "Keep it on him but let me handle this."

Scott's body was rigid. She grabbed for the gun at the same time Scott's right hand wrapped around her arm. Hard. The gun in her hand jiggled, but she kept her grip. She had the gun. He had her.

His eyes bulged, anger sizzling in his scowl. "Drop it." His voice wavered, but his grip was steel.

She pulled back, or at least she tried. He wasn't letting go. His eyes flicked from the gun in her hand to her face. The scowl never left his lips.

"Give me the gun." His voice gained force and his grip tightened. Shay slapped her left hand on the steering wheel as he yanked forward. Her back ached as he held her braced at an uncomfortable angle.

"Let go, Scott."

Another yank. "You let go."

Her heart beat double-time, but she wouldn't let him get the best of her. She could talk him down. She could get him to see reason. "Come on. You don't want to do this anymore. You're hurt. Let's get you medical attention and let's get out of this heat."

He gave her that scowl. "Fuck you. You and your boyfriend aren't getting out of this alive, bitch."

He pulled, and her forehead hit the hot metal of the SUV. Stars danced in her vision, but her grip stayed on the gun.

So far.

GARRET HELD the gun and heard every word coming from that asshole's mouth. He saw Shay's head jerk forward and hit the side of the car. Son of a bitch.

Shay shook her head and tried again. "Scott, let go and let's be done. The police are on their way. It's over."

Garret couldn't believe she was still trying to verbal judo her way out of this. The guy was an ass. He wasn't listening to reason. He wasn't in a normal frame of mind.

"It's not over, bitch." Scott lurched forward, pulling on Shay, who reared back as far as she could. She cocked her fist and let it fly—right into Scott's face. His head bounced and then he was still.

She drew away, keeping her eyes on the unmoving body. "Got cuffs?" She dragged Scott from his seat and set him—way too gently, in Garret's opinion—facedown on the side of the road, tugging his wrists behind his back.

Garret winced as he twisted to grab his cuffs from his belt and handed them to her. The damn ribs were getting worse.

"Are you okay?"

"Fine." He handed her the cuffs and fought off another wince. The pain in his ribs radiated down his legs and up his spine. "Don't worry about me, just take care of him."

"I got him." Shay snapped the cuffs around Scott's wrists. "Can you check on Sal and the woman? See if they need help over there."

"Sure." Garret nodded. The little movement made his stomach clench. His eyes barely focused on the wavy road and the splotches of cars coming toward him. *Just avoid the splotches.* He kept up that mantra as he crossed the road, like a tweaked-out Frogger.

Somehow, Garret dodged the traffic splotches and made it across the street. His eyes refocused as he got closer and closer to Lopez, whose hand was pressed against Sal's stomach.

Red seeped through the material in his hand, but Lopez held strong. "Stay with me, Sal. You still owe me a trip to that strip club in North Las Vegas. Don't think this little bee sting is going to get you off the hook."

Sal snorted and then grunted in pain. He was alive. Thank God.

"I want table service and a lap dance, dude." Lopez's hands didn't move. He might be a horn dog, but he was a good guy. And the little smile on Sal's face said Lopez and his strip club talk was distracting Sal from the pain. Good guy.

Garret's eyes moved to the woman, leaning against the car crying. Adam had his arm around her as he told her that she was safe and everything would be okay.

Everyone looked safe. Relatively speaking. Shay had the bad guy. Garret's gun was back in the good guy's custody. He wasn't needed anymore.

Garret knew the exact moment the adrenaline left his body. A sigh left his lips as his shoulders drooped. Knives danced in his chest, slashing up and down making it hard to move. His breath went choppy. His legs buckled. His ass went splat on the ground, next to Sal.

"Garret? Garret?" The voice calling him drew farther and farther away. He'd answer later. He was too tired to answer now. Later. His head fell back softly, like on a pillow. He didn't even feel the ground touch him.

He didn't feel anything anymore. He just heard his name, over and over again, and the sound of sirens. Yep. They'd all be taken care of. They didn't need him anymore.

CHAPTER TWENTY-SIX

TWENTY VERY LONG HOURS LATER, Shay walked through the hospital parking lot. Between the police interviews and getting checked out by the ambulance at the scene, they'd been stuck in the middle of the desert for way too long.

She was covered in sandy dust. Exhausted. She couldn't wait to take a long hot shower back at the hotel. But she had to do one thing first. She had to check on Garret.

Word at the crime scene was that he had a broken rib. He would be okay. But she had to see. She had to make sure.

Sliding glass doors split open and the alcohol smell of the hospital barreled through the door. She could do this. She hadn't been in a hospital since her parents—not really. She'd brought in a perp here or there but nothing like this. Nothing like seeing someone she loved in one of those beds—dying...

Loved. Fuck. And yes, she meant it. She was falling

hard for this man. What would happen if she were with him longer?

She shook her head and walked through the door. She didn't have time to freak out about relationships. Not while she was in a hospital. She could do this. Shay stopped at the information desk in the middle of the huge atrium. The name of the man she couldn't wait to see hung on her lips. But she didn't want to say it. Saying his name would make it real. Still, she said, "I'm looking for Garret Doyle's room."

"Sure. Relationship?"

They had a relationship and it was about to be gone. She'd go back to Chicago and he'd stay here. And she'd try not to regret her crazy vacation in Vegas. She was already regretting it. She was regretting the way her body throbbed when she thought about him. She was regretting the sharp ache in her chest when she thought of leaving him. "Friend."

"Okay. I'll look into that for you." The woman behind the desk punched in some information. Shay's heart thumped in her ears as she rubbed her clammy hands together. Finally, the woman looked up and smiled. "Here he is. Room 4422." She picked up a paper badge from the stack at the edge of her desk. She handed it to Shay. "Take those elevators to the third floor."

"What about Salvador Ruiz's room?" She wanted to see Sal, but she needed to see Garret.

The woman smiled and clicked-clacked on the keyboard. "Room 3438. Same elevators."

"Thank you." Shay tried to smile, but deep down

she was hoping they'd tell her he didn't have a room. That he was fine and sent home and she could say her good-byes from the comfort of his apartment. Not here.

She walked slowly to the elevators. Breathing in and out. She could do this. It was just a hospital. A big building. Nothing more.

She pressed the button for the elevator and stared out the atrium windows. The windows almost made it feel like she could escape. Run, if she had to. But she didn't have to. She could do this.

The elevator slid open and two women stepped off. The door gaped. She just had to walk in. Two steps— maybe three— tops. The door started to close. She could stop it. Or not.

Somebody slid past her, slipping inside the elevator. The door opened all the way again. "Coming in?" the guy in the elevator asked.

"Yeah." She attempted a common-courtesy smile, but she wasn't feeling it. She moved her lead feet. One step. Two steps. The door closed behind her. She turned and pressed floor four.

The elevator crawled. The lights in the ceiling combined with the metal walls were like an Easy-Bake Oven on steroids. Heat pooled and dripped down her back.

She wasn't sure if it was just her memory or if the antiseptic smell was pumped into the tiny hoist-coffin. The door opened, and the guy got off. Floor two. She had two more to go.

This was for Garret. She could do it. The elevator crept open on a big red 4 shouting from the wall across from her. She took two steps and looked for the signs with room directions. 4401-4424. To the right.

She walked, glancing in at people in various state of healing. 4406. Windows in the rooms poured light over the patients. Men and women she didn't know.

Nothing. She felt nothing. 4414. Her breathing slowly returned to normal. She could do this.

4422. Shay entered the room. Garret. His face a series of black and blue graffiti. A cut over his eye held together with Steri-Strips. His chest rose and fell. Heart monitors beeped.

The antiseptic smell filler her head. Stronger and stronger. Her heart hammered. Her breath stopped.

"Come inside and say your good-byes." An older woman with soft ebony hands leads fifteen-year-old Shay into the hospital room. Her mother's body is so still. The heart machine beeps. So. Slow. As if her heart struggles to take that next pump... Beep.

Shay grabs onto her mother's hand. What should she even say?

"Tell her anything you want her to know." The older woman must be reading her mind.

There's nothing she needs to tell her. Her mom is going to come home soon. The doctors just need to fix her. Do their job. "Don't leave me. Nip needs you. I need you."

Her mother's eye fly open as the beeping accelerates into screaming, angry pulses. Shay jumps, and the nurse pushes her off to the side. Her mom's waking up. Shay can see the honey of her mom's eyes. Her mom will fight.

She always said nothing could keep her away from her babies.

Doctors fly in the door. The erratic staccato of the beeping stops, turns into one long screech.

Nurses run into the room pushing a cart. Why are they running? Her mom is okay. Shay can see her eyes. It's all going to be okay.

Shay's eyes stayed on Garret, not seeing him. Outside. She just needed to see outside, the sun or the sky, but curtains covered the windows. Breathe. Her lungs sputtered as she tried to pull in any shred of oxygen. Her head spun.

"Shay?" Allison. Allison was here. "Are you okay?'

"I can't. I'm sorry. I can't." Shay stumbled over her own feet and tripped her way down the hall. She could feel Allison at her back. She didn't care. She needed out. Now.

"Shay, are you okay?" Allison caught up with her at the elevators.

"I can't do this." Shay hit the button for the elevator some thirty-seven times. Probably more. After that she lost count.

Allison's hand was stroking Shay's arm. "Garret's going to be okay."

"I can't do hospitals."

Tears lined Allison's eyes. "Yeah. They're hard for me too." Allison would know. Something about seeing your parents die when you were young ruined the whole hospital experience.

Shay hit the down button again. "Tell him goodbye."

"Don't you want to tell him yourself?"

The door flew open and Shay jumped in. "I can't." She pressed the button for the ground floor. "Please."

"I'll tell him." Allison's lips curved into a smile that didn't match the tears in her eyes.

"Thank you." The doors closed on the memories and on her chance to say good-bye.

GARRET'S CHEST was wrapped in a vise. His head hurt. But none of that mattered.

Oranges. He could smell her. The soft skin of her hand was on his. He'd felt her hand the whole time he was out. He'd had the most amazing dreams about orchards and breakfast—and Shay had been at the center of them all.

With just her touch, he knew everything was going to be okay.

His eyes focused on the woman next to him. Not Shay. Allison? "Hi," his throat scraped out.

"Oh, thank goodness you're okay." She squeezed his hand tighter. "We've been so worried."

"Nice to have you back, buddy." Byrnes leaned over the bed and held up a hand for a high-five. "How are you feeling?"

Garret lifted his arm, but couldn't reach. Spikes dragged along his chest. "Like shit." It wasn't a lie. Raising his hand was the equivalent of getting kicked in the ribs. Again.

"You look like shit too, so there's that."

"There is that." Garret laughed. Mistake. His chest stopped shaking immediately and he regretted ever finding anything amusing. "How long have I been out?"

"Since yesterday."

"How long have you been here?"

"About the same. We didn't want you to wake up alone." Allison's stare moved to the wall, the floor, anywhere but at him. "She tried."

She being Shay. "When did she leave?" He tried to sit up in the bed, but the compression tape on his chest made it impossible to move.

"She couldn't come in the room. It was too hard."

She couldn't come in. And she was gone. She was leaving for Chicago.

"I just wanted to say thank you." Allison looked at some paperwork in her hands. "Thank you for finding Julie's necklace, and even more so, thank you for bringing Adam and my friends back alive. I don't know what I would have done if I had lost any one of them— or you or Sal. But somehow you all made it back, and I heard you were a big part of that. So, thank you."

Sal. What kind of crappy friend was he? He hadn't asked about Sal. "You don't have to thank me. We just did our job. How's Sal doing?"

"I just saw him. The bullet missed anything important, so the doctor is sure he'll be fine." She smiled, but something was on her mind. She couldn't seem to look him in the eyes. "Anyway, you did more than your job. I'm sure that's why Shay likes you so much."

Was Allison going to start passing notes? Was that what this was? Not that he'd complain. If Shay was trying to reach out to him, no matter how juvenile, he'd take it. "Shay sent you?"

Her smile dimmed. "No. She decided to head to the airport early."

She'd left? Just left. No good-bye. Nothing. His chest ached just a little bit more with that information. She hadn't waited to see him. She hadn't stuck around.

"I hope you can understand. It's the hospital... and life. She's lost everyone, and she's losing so much more with her brother."

Byrne's rested his arm on Allison's shoulder. "Why don't you ask him?"

"Oh, yeah." Allison's smile went full wattage. Garret wasn't sure if that grin was for him or for her fiancé. He had a feeling it was for Byrnes.

She was cute. He could see what the man saw in her. Between her look, the way she talked, the way she adored Byrnes. She was perfect for him. Maybe one day he'd find something like that. He tried not to think about how he had. How she'd walked away and was running straight to the airport.

"We're getting married this weekend. We know it's short notice and Chicago is a long way from Vegas, but we'd love to have you there. We invited Sal, but with his injuries, he probably won't be able to fly."

"I don't know." Garret wasn't ready to make any commitments. Especially commitments that would put him in the path of Shay. She'd just left. He understood she wasn't a fan of hospitals, but she could have waited. But she didn't.

Allison looked down at the paper in her hands. "That sounds like a no."

"Honey, it sounds like he has to see if he feels up to it." Byrnes squeezed her shoulder and kissed the top of her head. "The guy broke a rib. He needs to get his rest."

"I know, but I'm so thankful for everything you've done and I can't thank you enough for keeping everyone safe." She smiled. "Here's an invitation and a plane ticket. I really hope you can be there. Shay wants you there."

"Allison." Byrnes shook his head.

"What? She does want him there. She's just stubborn and afraid to get hurt."

Garret held this laugh inside where it wouldn't shove daggers into his chest. Shay wasn't the type to be afraid of anything.

"You've said enough." Byrnes put a hand over his bride's mouth. "This is going to be the shortest wedding on record if Shay finds out you're playing matchmaker." Byrnes' hand jerked back. She must have bitten him. Good. She was full of good information. Just keep it coming.

"I'm good at this." Allison started to pout. "Look at Brook and Joe. That was all me, Adam."

"You had nothing to do with that." Byrnes laughed.

"Indirectly."

"What makes you think she'd want me at the wedding?" Garret didn't want to hear about Brook and Perretti. Not right now. He had only one person on his mind.

Byrnes laughed. "Really? That woman was a wreck when you passed out on the side of the road. She fought with the EMTs when she thought they weren't moving fast enough. She harassed the doctors for information. Hell, I think she told them she was your fiancée so they'd even talk to her on the phone." He sighed and looked at Allison. "See, now you have me doing it."

Her grin was all pride and arrogance. She knew exactly what he was doing. And she knew she encouraged it.

"Shay called the hospital." Could they be right? Could Shay want him at the wedding? Could she want him in her life? Could she want a half-relationship with him in Vegas and her in Chicago?

"She did." Allison preened.

So she wasn't running away, but did that really change anything? "The long-distance thing never works." He was lying. He'd consider doing the whole long-distance—daily phone call, video chat, phone sex —thing with her. He'd consider anything to have her.

"I can't believe I'm saying this." Byrnes shook his head. "Aren't your parents in Montana? What's keeping you here?"

Allison practically bounced. "Exactly. It's not like I own a jewelry company that's always looking for security. Hell, my head of security is like nine thousand years old. He has more vacation time than actually working days in a year. He's ready to retire. We just haven't pushed it. Say the word and he's relaxing on a beach in Mexico."

"Ummm..." It's not like her offer wasn't nice, but he

really didn't want to be a figurehead. His job at Pura Vida was exciting and different. They probably didn't get a bunch of drunk and disorderlies at a jewelry company.

"All right, let's give Garret a break so he can rest. He doesn't even know if he can travel in his condition." Byrnes held Allison's shoulders to keep her from bouncing. "We've done enough damage here. Let's go."

"Fine." She frowned and headed for the door. She turned before she reached the hall. "No matter what, I hope you come to the wedding. If the doctor will let you, anyway. I really do appreciate everything you did for us here." She disappeared.

Adam Byrnes stayed behind. "I'd really like you to come, if you're well enough." He slapped Garret on the shoulder.

Everything throbbed. "Dick."

Adam laughed. "Allison doesn't know this, but the doctor said you could travel."

Garret didn't know why Byrnes would be asking about Garret's travel plans, but the look on his face must have been enough because Adam said, "Shay asked when she called."

Shay wanted to know if he could fly? Interesting.

"So, if you wanted, you could come. If Allison knew, she'd never leave until you agreed to fly out. So, you're welcome."

"That's your woman." Garret laughed as a goofy grin overtook Adam's face. And Byrnes somehow had become a friend.

"Yes, she is." Byrnes tapped Garret's shoulder again. "And if you're smart, I'll see you this weekend."

Then he was gone.

Garret leaned against the pillow and closed his eyes. The silence of the room should have felt lonely, but it didn't. It gave him time to think.

If he was smart...

If he was smart, he would follow Shay and the way she made him feel. If he was smart, he never would have started anything with Shay, knowing she was going to disappear from his life. If he was smart...

He'd never been smart.

CHAPTER TWENTY-SEVEN

GARRET TOOK a ragged breath as he walked through the Pura Vida's atrium. The hospital had just discharged him. He should be heading back to his apartment, but he couldn't do it. The thought of sitting there alone doing nothing was the equivalent of a nightmare.

"Garret? What are you doing here?" Viola's heels clicked on the tile.

"I thought I'd see how things are going." Crap. He knew he'd get backlash for coming in so quickly after what happened.

"You should be home resting." She sighed and shook her head. "But you won't do that, will you?" She didn't wait for him to answer. She just pointed toward the back office. "Fine. Follow me, we need to talk."

What everyone wanted to hear from their boss.

He followed her past the front counter and down a hall. He didn't visit this part of the hotel very often. He didn't have an office back here, and management came to him for the most part. After all, his department had the best cameras.

The huge window in Viola's office looked out over the zoo and water park. The furniture was light wood, and doilies covered every surface. When he'd first walked in, his impression was this was not exactly what he thought her office would look like. But it fit her.

"Want a drink?" Viola had never offered him a drink before.

He didn't know if that meant what was coming was a good thing or a bad thing. Since she had already poured herself a glass and was taking a sip, he could assume it was bad.

"Is this a conversation where I'm going to need one?"

After refilling her glass she poured another one, and set it on her desk in front of Garret. "Have a seat."

This was not good. But for the life of him, he couldn't figure out why. And he did not like playing these games. "Should I clean out my desk?"

"No. No." She smiled. "Garret, how are you feeling?"

"Fine. I'd feel better if I knew what was going on."

She sighed. "I'm sorry. This is hard for me." She took a long sip. "First. I want to tell you, you are an amazing asset to my team. You pulled off a miracle with the awards show. I'm not the only one that noticed. We're opening another hotel, and they want you to help get the security set up."

"Leave Pura Vida."

"Yes. It's a promotion. More money. But you'd be

spending your time at the new hotel until it's up and running."

"What happens after that?" Leave Pura Vida? He'd thought about leaving for Shay. But he wasn't sure if she'd even want him. And here Viola was, offering him the opportunity he'd always wanted. This was it. Exactly what he was trained for. He could build a career around setting up hotels in Vegas.

"That's up to you. There's talk of expansion over the next ten years. You could easily fit into that niche."

"Where's the new hotel?"

"That's where things get tricky—or exciting, depending on how you want to look at it. Madrid, Spain."

"Wow."

"Yeah, wow." Viola nodded. "We'll miss you, but I won't stand in your way. This is huge for your career. They were really impressed with how you kept everything under control at the awards."

He laughed. "I honestly thought you were going to fire me for what happened with Rick Drakos."

"That was unfortunate, and we need to discuss how to ensure nothing like that happens again, but it wasn't your fault. That blame falls soundly on the firm that does your background checks."

"Why are you telling me about all of this? Shouldn't it come from my bosses at the security firm?"

"Yeah normally it would, but I asked if I could deliver the news." Her face took on a wistful expression. "I'm going to miss you."

"I haven't taken the job, yet."

She smiled. "You will. You're a smart man. This could set you up."

Why did everyone assume he was a smart man? If the last week had taught him anything, he was the furthest thing from smart. "Thanks, Viola. I'll give you my answer by tomorrow."

"Are you sure you don't want to wait until after this weekend?" She smiled. "I spoke to Allison Southby. She mentioned you'll be seeing a certain Chicago cop."

He didn't want to talk about this. Not with her, not with anyone. He hadn't figured out what to do about Shay. Dammit. "It doesn't change anything. It really just makes it worse. I'll be in a different country and she'll be in Chicago." He ran a hand through his hair, rubbing the pain that landed in his neck. "She just left. She didn't even say good-bye. Why should I ask her what she thinks I should do?"

"Do you like her?"

Of course he did. He was picturing a future with her. He was picturing everything with her. "It's been a week." Which was why he felt so stupid. "You don't make life decisions based on one week."

"No. But if you really want to see where this is going to go, then you do whatever you can to fit her into your life. You don't have to stop your life just make room."

He walked toward the door. "Thanks."

"No problem, and stay out of my hotel. You're on leave."

"On leave?"

"To heal." Viola smiled. "Have a safe trip to Chicago."

Every piece of his body and soul wanted to take the next flight out. Every beat of his heart knew where it belonged. And it wasn't here. It wasn't in Vegas. Nothing really tied him here anymore. Just his job. But he could always find another one of those. Right?

He'd never find another Shay. But did she even want him to find her?

SHAY CARRIED another box out of the house and put it in Shawn's Jeep. "Do you really need this?" She pulled out a Darth Vader bobblehead.

"Yes. It helps me relax." Shawn pushed the toy back in the box and covered it with a stack of clothes.

"Are you sure you don't want a suitcase?"

"I'm sure. There's nowhere to put it once I'm in the dorm."

"So the bobblehead gets a box, but your clothes are just thrown in the back?"

Shawn grabbed another armload of clothes from the front porch and shoved them in the back seat. "Yes, now you understand."

"I don't understand."

Shawn shoved the door closed against the mountain of clothes. "I'm going to miss you, sis." He wrapped his arms around her.

She crushed him to her and the tears brewed in her eyes.

"You're squishing me." His voice sounded strained.

"Sorry, Nip." She pulled away. "I'm just going to miss you." All the things they'd done together, all the things she'd wanted to do, everything ran through her mind. She'd always thought they'd have more time. And now he was off to college.

She wrapped her arms around him again and held on. Maybe if she didn't let go, he wouldn't leave. Or couldn't leave. She was okay either way.

"You're killing me." He tried to get away.

"I don't want you to leave me."

He pulled her closer. "I can come back every weekend." The guilt in his voice was hard to miss. And the selfish in her voice caused it. She was an adult, who taught him to be an adult.

She pulled away and smoothed his t-shirt. "Don't be silly. You don't need to come back. I'll be just fine." Shay smiled and she made sure it radiated all the joy and happiness it should convey. "But be back for Thanksgiving."

"Of course." Shawn leaned in for another hug.

"Now go, before you're driving in the dark."

Shawn jogged around to the driver's side door. "Thanks, Shay."

"Drive safely, Nip."

Then his car was gone, rolling down the block and heading for the interstate. Most of his stuff, gone. What wasn't gone was beer. She needed one.

She trudged through the house to the kitchen and opened the refrigerator. Picking up a bottle, Shay shut the door. A piece of paper hung in front of her face.

Out with Clive. Don't wait up. In her gran's squiggly little writing. She was alone.

She sat at the kitchen table and absorbed silence. No one asking questions. No one needing her. She didn't know what to do with herself.

"Oh, there you are." Her gran hobbled in the back door.

"I thought you went out with Clive."

"Forgot my bathing suit. I offered to go skinny dipping, but his grandchildren might be there so we didn't think that was the best time for nudie-swimming."

"Good call." Although was there ever a good time for nudie-swimming in one's eighties?

"Nip leave?"

"Yep." Shay took a drink of the beer in her hands.

"Maybe you should call that man of yours."

"What man?" She hadn't told her gran about Garret. She didn't want an I-told-you-so, unsolicited advice, or anything else that usually came from her gran's meddling.

"I'm not blind. I know you've been pining for a man for the past few days."

"How could you know that?" Shay shook her head at how that sounded—like she was pining. "Because I'm not."

"Brook told me."

Perretti's girlfriend stayed at the house last year when her life was in danger, and Brook and Gran had formed a friendship. Shay thought it was cute at the time. Now? Not so much. "Don't listen to everything Brook tells you."

"But she's right about this." Gran sat down at the table and patted Shay's arm. "You love this boy."

Shay felt like a teenager talking about what boy she had a crush on. But this was so much more than that. "I could."

"Then you should call him."

"He lives in Vegas. I live here." Shay tried to smile, something that would say she was okay with the situation. It's not like she had control. But she couldn't even look at Gran while she spouted that bullshit. She had control and she'd made her choice. "It doesn't exactly add up to a successful relationship."

A loud crash came from across the table. Shay jumped in her seat and met her gran's angry stare. "What the hell, Gran?"

"What the hell, Shay?" Gran shook her head. "I've failed you. I thought I raised you to be a strong woman. To go after what you want. But here you are sitting around, alone."

"I'm not alone. I have you."

"Missy, I am eighty-three years old. I'm not going to be around forever. Nip is going off to college and then he'll have his own career, his own life." Gran patted Shay's arm again. "I appreciate everything you did to take care of your brother and I over the years. But we're grown now. We have our own lives. You need to find your own life too."

Shay played with her gran's fingers. It felt so good to have here, but she was right. Gran had a life. Shay needed one. And the only person she could see in that life was Garret. "He's never going to talk to me again. I ran away."

"You ran away?"

"He was in the hospital." That was all Shay had to say for the sympathy to wash across her gran's face. Gran knew. She'd been there when it all went down. Her gran had always been there.

"You don't know if he'll talk until you try." Gran squeezed her hand. "And you will try. I didn't raise a quitter."

She didn't want to quit. "But he lives so far."

"You afraid of planes now? You ain't heard of phones?" Gran pulled her hand away. "No more excuses, young lady. If you want to be alone and miserable, go ahead and buy an assortment of housecoats and give up. But if you want to live your life, quit your bellyaching and get your man."

"What if he doesn't want me?"

"Then he's a dummy. And you don't want no dummy. You already married one of those. You hit your quota."

Garret's face flashed in front of Shay. His smile. The way he pushed her. The way she pushed back. She was with him for barely a week. She'd been away from him for a couple days. And it felt like an eternity.

She didn't care about the distance. She didn't care about any of it. She just wanted to hear his voice. Her spine stiffened. She could do this. "I'll call him."

Gran smiled and slowly lifted herself from the kitchen chair. "I knew my granddaughter was in there somewhere." She turned her head back and forth. "I forgot why I'm in here." She headed down the hall. "Maybe I'll pretend to forget, so I can go skinny dipping."

"The grandkids will be there. Don't you dare."

Gran's cackle echoed off the walls. Whether it was a cackle that said she'd never do that or a cackle that said she'd already forgotten her suit and was planning the unveiling of her birthday suit, Shay had no idea. For her own sanity, she chose not to find out.

Anyway, she had things to do. People to call. Well, one person to call. She picked up her cell phone and dialed the number. Got voicemail.

Shit.

CHAPTER TWENTY-EIGHT

THE HOUR-LONG WEDDING service was a nightmare. Shay had stood there like a good little bridesmaid in her floofy dress, with those high-heeled torture devices strapped to her feet. She thought once the service was over, she'd get to sit down—maybe get a drink. Adam promised her an open bar at the reception. But nope. There was no sitting, and no drinking.

After the service, there were an obscene amount of pictures. Under a tree, next to a tree, without a tree. They'd taken pictures alone, together, and every which way the group could be sliced.

And when that was done, she thought—foolishly—it was time to rest. Bring on the sitting and the drinking. Nope. Now they stood outside the backyard in a receiving line greeting everyone at the wedding. All one hundred guests. This was the new definition of hell.

If she was asked one more time how she knew the bride, she'd flip. If she had to watch the shock pass over one more face when she told them she was a cop, she might hurl. Heck, if she had to say "I work with Adam at the Chicago Police Department," one more time she might string herself up by the tulle and lace wrapped around her hips.

Birds chirped off in the distance as Julie smiled at her. Okay fine, maybe she was a tad cranky. She needed to get over it. Today was a beautiful day.

The arboretum was still under water, as well as most of the county. Hell, even the retention pond down the road was more a retention lake at this point. But Adam's mother's yard was dry as a bone. She'd hired some landscapers to dry it out, whatever that meant. Rich people.

The sun was shining, the ground was dry and the wedding was beautiful. Yet Shay was still in a gnarly mood. She'd left Vegas four days ago.

Four days and Garret still hadn't contacted her. She'd called the hospital and found out he was released the day after she'd left for Chicago. That had been an interesting phone call. In order to get information, she had to remind them she was his fiancée. Which was fine, except they were confused why his fiancée didn't know that he was home.

Yeah. Take a number. She was confused, too.

She thought he'd call. She thought he'd miss her. But apparently not. It hurt. And it wasn't like he was holed up in some hospital room unable to call her. He was home, choosing not to.

She dropped her head and stared at her shoes. She was not going to cry. She might not know ninety-eight percent of people at this wedding, but she knew a few. And if her eyes started dripping, she'd never hear the end of it.

"So, how do you know the bride?" a deep voice asked. If it wasn't asking her the most annoying question on earth, she might actually find the voice sexy.

"I'm friends with the bride." She painted that happy smile on her face and lifted her head. "but I work with Adam at..."

Garret.

He looked really good in a black suit. His red shirt brought out his tan and the green in his eyes. You couldn't even tell what happened in Vegas. He looked good. He looked good enough to sit on. For like, rest, nothing kinky.

Although, thoughts of Garret and kinky weren't all that bad...

Wait. It was that bad. He hadn't called. He was here because he was now besties with Joe and Adam.

"Hi. I'm glad you could make it." She smiled. She was sure of it. She was giving an Academy Award-winning performance here. And the Oscar goes to...

"I wouldn't miss it."

She nodded. Of course he wouldn't. Like she thought, him and Adam were now besties. Funny how Garret could manage to keep a friend who lived across the country, but not a girlfriend. Nope. She wasn't worth the airline miles.

Okay, that wasn't funny ha-ha. That was more funny tragic.

"I didn't think this would be so hard," Garret said.

Shay didn't have time for tragic. "What's hard?"

"Seeing you."

Seeing her was hard? What was hard about it? Probably having to face her after not calling—having to face her when he was hoping he'd never have to see her again. "Fine. Let me make this easy for you." She tapped Julie on the shoulder. "I'm taking a break." She turned back to Garret. "Now you don't have to see me." That last part came out a little too harsh and right in Garret's face. Seeing him after everything they'd been through wasn't exactly high on her list either.

She didn't wait for a response from Julie or him. She didn't care. She turned and left—left the receiving line and left the yard. She walked around the sprawling mansion until she was on the road and out of sight of the house. It was a power move—well, it would have been if she didn't trip every dozen steps because of the torture devices on her feet.

She leaned against one of the cars lining the side of the road. Cars stretched along the street for miles. Her car was somewhere in that mess, but thanks to the valets, she wasn't quite sure where.

Okay, now she wanted to cry. But why?

She didn't want to be the social little bridesmaid anyway. Now she had a reason to leave. Except she didn't know where her car was, and her gran and Gran's boyfriend were somewhere in the yard roaming the party.

Shit. She couldn't really leave.

But there was a bright side. At least Garret wasn't

in her face looking all concerned because he didn't want to hurt her feelings.

What a crappy silver lining.

SO...

This hadn't worked out the way Garret thought it would. He thought she'd be happy to see him. He thought she'd run into his arms and...and... oh hell, who knew what he thought she'd do. But he could honestly say he didn't think she'd run the other way.

"Are you going to just stand there, or are you going to go after her?" Julie stood there staring at him. Like he was an idiot. He was an idiot. He came all this way and she'd just walked away—no, ran. Again. And Shay didn't look like she wanted to see him.

He hated to admit it, but standing there was starting to sound like a good idea.

Julie tapped her high-heeled foot. "Well?"

Well what? Why should he go after her? He came here for one reason, to support Adam and Allison.

Okay, two reasons. He came here for two reasons. And that other reason was running away from him. He couldn't let her get away. He'd come this far to see her, and he wasn't about to give up that easy.

He made his way through the guests and out to the front of the house. Knowing Shay, she was probably halfway to Mexico by now. Or not. He found her next to the string of cars lining the street, her hip against an SUV, her head hanging down.

"Shay?"

She turned around, and heaven help him, he could see tears in her eyes.

"Are you okay?" His heart actually broke just watching her.

She stiffened her spine and turned on that fake-ass high-wattage smile. "What would be wrong?"

"Do you want to tell me why you're running away from me?"

"What makes you think this is about you? I'm not running away from you. I needed some air."

"Outside?"

She sighed. "Yes. That is where the air is."

"Weren't you outside in the backyard too? Or is that different outside air?"

"Look, Garret. You wanted your space, I'm giving it to you. I can't leave. I'm in too deep. Go say your congrats and whatever else you're here to do and go. Then we can all go our separate ways and things can go back to normal."

"Okay."

"Okay." She turned away from him.

"What if I don't want to go back to normal?" He'd done normal for over thirty years. Normal sucked. The time he'd spent with Shay had been some of the best times he'd had in a really long time.

"Garret..."

"No." He moved closer. His hand itched to touch her. "I'm not letting you push me away again."

"Me push you away?" She took a step closer. Not in a nice, sweet let's play doctor kind of way. She looked ready to take him down. "I didn't push you away."

"You left without saying goodbye."

"It was the hospital. I haven't been inside one since my parents died." Shay pulled in a large breath. "I couldn't stay. I'm sorry."

"I figured that, plus Allison told me."

"If you figured that, then why haven't you been answering my calls?"

"I was heading to Chicago." Garret took a hesitant step toward her. He couldn't stand being this close and not touching. But she had to want it. "Why did you call me?"

"I..." Shay's body tensed, eyes on the side of the road.

"You what?"

"I wanted to hear your voice and see if you were still interested in me. I know you're in Chicago and I'm in Vegas... Wait. I'm in Chicago and you're in Vegas." Shay was tripping over her words, and it was damn adorable. "And it's far. But I didn't know if we could make this work long distance—hell—if you'd even want to make this work long distance."

If he'd want to? At least it meant she'd thought about it. Maybe there was a chance she wanted to make this work after all. "What if I said I did? I did want to try."

"Your life is in Vegas." She shook her head. "My life is here. I could never ask you to give up the career you've built, for me. And I can't just leave. I have Gran and my brother."

"What if I said I don't care about my job or career or any of it?" He hadn't meant to say that, but now, standing here inches from Shay, he knew he meant it. He didn't care about any of it. Jobs were everywhere. There was only one Shay.

"Garret..."

"Shay." He stepped closer to her and rested a hand on the side of her face. Her skin was so soft and so warm. God, she was beautiful.

Her eyes closed as he rubbed his thumb back and forth along her cheek. A small groan came from deep inside her. He couldn't hold back any longer. He rested his lips on hers. Soft, sweet kisses that tasted like peppermint. She even tasted beautiful.

He pulled back but didn't move his hand from her face. He couldn't stop touching her if he wanted to. And he didn't want to. "What if I said I don't care where I am, as long as you're with me?"

She smiled. A real smile, not the crap she tried to pull off earlier. "I'd say you must have gotten that line from a romance novel, because no one talks like that."

He laughed. This woman. She was maddening and adorable. And if he played his cards right—his. "I talk like that."

She put her hands on his chest. He tried not to wince. His rib was still healing. He'd managed to get through the flight by not moving and not lifting his arms. But even a little pressure made his breath stutter.

She pulled away. "I'm sorry. I forgot about your ribs."

He just wanted her to touch him again. Anywhere.

Preferably not on his ribs, but he was desperate. He moved toward her and she stepped back.

Disappointment balled in his throat. Why did he even bother trying? It always ended the same. He ended up alone and miserable and trying to pick up the pieces when he didn't even want to keep going. He dropped his hand from her skin like it was on fire. "I should probably go."

He had to leave before he starting crying like a baby. How pathetic. He'd never cried over a woman before. Now he was on the verge of becoming a fountain of misery.

"So, do you need a place to stay?" Shay wrapped her hand around the collar of his shirt, not touching his ribs and not letting him leave.

"Tonight?" He would love to have one more for the road, but as this whole interaction proved, he couldn't handle it.

"Tonight? Tomorrow? When you come back?"

"I can't do another one-night stand with you." Although calling what they'd had a one-night stand wasn't exactly appropriate. But fling or tryst didn't seem to fit either.

"Who said anything about one night?" She smiled.

"Does that mean we're giving us a try?"

Shay shifted her feet and glanced off to the side. "Um..."

He loved watching this normally unrufflable woman ruffle. He'd like to think it was because of him. He'd like to think he had the same effect on her that she had on him. And maybe he did.

"Say it." He set his hands on her hips and pulled her body close to his. So fucking close. Having her near him was more important than any pain in his chest. "Tell me."

"Yes. I want to give us a try." It was like she whispered through him. The lump in his throat dissolved and his body relaxed. She wanted this. She wanted him.

His lips found hers. Soft was gone. Sweet, too. This was hunger and desire. He couldn't get enough of her as his hands roamed up and down her body. Mostly down. His ribs hurt when they roamed up.

"Um, Shay?" a voice called out and Shay jumped back, away from Garret. "They need you at the head table."

An older woman stood next to the car, her eyes crinkling with laughter. "You must be Garret."

Shay rolled her eyes and flattened out her dress with her hands. "Gran, this is Garret. Garret, this is my gran."

"It's nice to meet you. I've heard a lot about you." He offered his hand and Gran took it. She held on too long and inspected his fingers.

"I've heard quite a bit too." There was a twinkle in the old woman's eyes that made Garret smile. She looked like trouble with a capital mischief. He was going to like her. He could tell. "No ring. Nice solid hands. I like him."

"Gran."

"What? I just wanted to see the man you've been talking about for the last few days."

"She's been talking about me?" Garret couldn't help the hopeful lilt in his voice. She'd missed him. And she'd talked about him. That was something. "What did she say?"

"*He doesn't call.*" Gran narrowed her eyes. "I told her his phone must be broken. If he's as great as she says, he must be smart enough to see what a wonderful woman my Shay is."

"I do see. That's why I'm here."

"I knew you were smart and I hadn't even met you." Gran stood on tiptoes and patted his cheek.

He really liked this woman. She was kind, but there was a ferociousness under the surface. She cared about Shay. And so did he. "I was wondering if her phone was broken, too."

"I called," Shay muttered.

"Calling the hospital and pretending to be my fiancée does not count."

"You knew about that?"

"Well, Shay, you've been holding out." Gran howled with laughter.

"Gran, go back to your date." Shay sighed. "I'll be there in just a minute."

"You never let me have any fun." Gran turned and headed back toward the backyard.

Once Gran was out of hearing distance, Shay looked at Garret. "Are you sure about moving here? She's my gran. I've invested this much time in her. I can't really get rid of her now."

"Absolutely." He smiled and pressed a kiss to her

forehead. "She's an amazing woman. I think we'll get along."

"I'm sure you will." Her face went from smile to horror-stricken. "But then there's Shawn..."

He tugged on her arm until she was facing him. "I'm sure I'll love him. Stop trying to talk me out of this. It's you. Shayleigh, you're it for me. You're the one."

Her lips curved into the most delicious smile. That, paired with her in high-heels and that dress. He was so turned on and there wasn't a damn thing he could do about it.

"You're the one for me, too." She laid a gentle kiss on his lips. And right then, he couldn't remember ever being this happy. Ever. And he knew it was Shay and he'd never let her go.

EXTRAS

Thank you for supporting an independent author. It would be great if you could leave a review or a rating wherever you purchased this book, or on Goodreads.

Would you like to know when my next book is available? You can sign up for my new release email list at http://www.vanessamknight.com or like my Facebook page at http://facebook.com/vanessamknightau thor.

ABOUT THE AUTHOR

Vanessa M. Knight has always enjoyed writing, and once she found mystery and romance, she was addicted. She props her laptop in the suburbs of Chicago with her family and menagerie of four-pawed claw-babies (AKA cats and dogs.) That laptop has part-nered in-crime to write contemporary romances with a dash of humor and splash of snark.

When she has a few moments to spare, you can find her singing off-key (but she assures everyone it's still considered singing), reading, kickboxing, or killing a few brain cells as she stares at the many sitcoms and dramas available through the Internet and TV.

For more information on Vanessa, including her Internet haunts, contest updates, and details on her upcoming novels, please visit her website at www.-vanessamknight.com.

Chicago's Finest Series

Second Time's the Charm

Stark Raving Mad

Stealing Vegas

Final Strike

Busted Series

Busting In

Busting Out

Busting Through

And look for her Contemporary New Adult series:

Ritter University Series

Major Renovations

What Happens in College...

Christmas Breakdown

Rushing In

Sophomore Slump

The Make-up Test

www.ingramcontent.com/pod-product-compliance
Lightning Source LLC
Chambersburg PA
CBHW061146210726
48294CB00006B/1591